W9-BON-019

OVER THE MOON

THE NOVELIZATION

Adapted by

Wendy Wan-Long Shan

Illustrations by

Glen Keane, Yujia Wang, Brittany Myers,
Jin Kim, Steven MacLeod, Edwin Rhemrev, Wang Rui,
Hikari Toriumi, Elle Shi, and *Tian Yuan*

HARPER
An Imprint of HarperCollinsPublishers

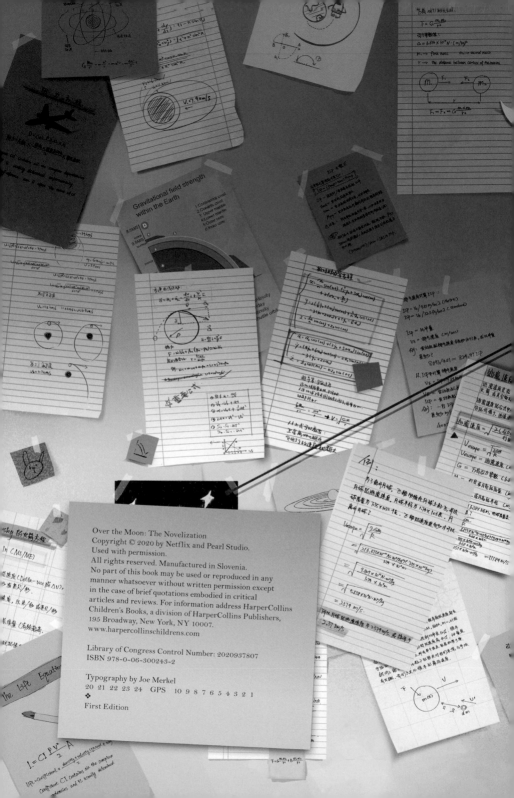

Library of Congress Control Number: 2020937807
ISBN 978-0-06-300243-2

Typography by Joe Merkel
20 21 22 23 24   GPS   10 9 8 7 6 5 4 3 2 1
❖
First Edition

Pronunciation Guide

Chang'e (chong-uh)

Fei Fei (fay fay)

Gobi (go-bee)

Houyi (ho-yee)

Mei (may)

Zhong (zōng)

Foreword

It seems to me that the best things in life are a gift . . . something you weren't expecting but when you receive it, it changes you for the better. When I first read Audrey Wells's draft of *Over the Moon*, I knew that it was something special. It was, in a sense, a gift—this very personal story from Audrey had as much emotion as it did fun. Fei Fei's journey would inevitably resonate across generations and cultures.

I love characters who believe the impossible is possible. They are the heroes and heroines who inspire our lives. Early on in my career, I was told by my mentor that the secret to animation is sincerity. At first, I didn't grasp what that meant, but eventually I understood it to mean "believe in your characters." In the case of Fei Fei, this girl is real to me. In *Over the Moon* we see what she sees and feel what she feels. She is smart, fearless, and through

her adventures, we learn a deeper meaning of love.

In preparation for telling this story, our team visited an ancient water town in China, with its quaint canals and bridges. It brought Fei Fei's world to life for our artists who created the beautiful art that inspired the illustrations in this book.

My hope is that while reading this story you find inspiration to encourage you on your own journey.

GLEN KEANE

Prologue

When Fei Fei was five, she saw two moons at once.
One moon was up in the sky, and then its reflection
shimmered in the water. When the water rippled,
the moon rippled, too. How wonderful to have not
one moon but two! Fei Fei, Mama, and Baba sat by
the canal, having a picnic. It was their special place
to be together.

"Scientists can tell us many things about space,"
said Mama. She leaned back and gestured to the
sky. Fei Fei loved looking at her mother's hands;
they could do anything, it seemed—tell a story,
wipe away a tear, make mooncakes. "They can tell
us how much the moon weighs. They can tell us
how far away the stars are. They can tell us that
space starts one hundred kilometers above the
Earth. But"—Mother leaned over—"they can't tell

us about Space Dog." Mother held her hand up in the sky, opening and closing it like the jaws of a dog, pretending to take a bite out of the moon. It was a trick of the eye, to see Mama's hand look almost as big as the moon. According to Mama, the Space Dog took bites out of the moon, causing the moon to slowly change shape.

"So, when the moon is big and round, that's when Space Dog doesn't take a bite?" asked Fei Fei. She imagined how the moon might look like a delicious cookie to a dog.

"That's when the moon goddess, Chang'e, makes him spit it out," said Mama. "Bleh!" Mama and Fei Fei collapsed into giggles.

"All right, does anyone want to hear the scientific explanation?" asked Baba. Baba liked answers that made sense, that were grounded in reality, rather than talk about Space Dog. He drew out the word "sci-en-ti-fic" but in a playful way. This was one of their family jokes, having scientific ideas battle creative stories. Fei Fei did like understanding ideas

scientifically, like her dad, and had the number one rank in her class to prove it. But she also enjoyed her mother's stories about how the world worked. Both versions of the world made it complete.

"Sorry, Baba, I like the Mommy explanation best!" said Fei Fei, giving her father an affectionate look.

"Outnumbered," said Mama to Baba, teasing him with a smile. He smiled back.

"Tell me about Chang'e," asked Fei Fei. She held up her Chang'e doll and waved it around. "Tell me, Mama?" Fei Fei loved hearing about the moon goddess.

"Again?" asked Baba. He sounded a little disappointed. He had probably been hoping to talk about constellations or the Milky Way, rather than Chang'e.

"Chang'e is kind and gentle. Her voice is as lovely as a flute's." Mama began the story of the moon goddess the same way every time. "And when she cries, her tears turn into stardust."

"Why does she cry?" asked Fei Fei, even though she already knew the answer.

"Because she lives on the moon, and she misses the love of her life, Houyi." As Mama said the last part, she untied a scarf from around her neck. When she held up the scarf, Fei Fei could see an image of Chang'e on it. Chang'e was beautiful and elegant; her robes floated around her as if she was so lovely she could not be touched.

"Long ago," said Mama, "beautiful and kind Chang'e and a handsome man named Houyi were in love."

"True love?" asked Fei Fei.

"True love," confirmed Mama. Mama repeated the story of their true love for Fei Fei, even though Fei Fei knew the story by heart. Houyi was a famed archer. The emperor on Earth at that time was Yao, and during his reign, ten suns burned in the sky and scorched the Earth. Yao asked Houyi to shoot them down to save the people.

Houyi went to the top of Kunlun Mountain and

used his magic bow to shoot down nine of the suns. The Jade Empress gave Houyi two immortality pills as a prize. After he shot down the nine suns, Houyi became very famous and received many apprentices, including one named Feng Meng. But Feng Meng went to Houyi's home and threatened Chang'e to give him the pills. Chang'e swallowed the two pills and floated to the moon, leaving Houyi devastated and alone on Earth. Every year Houyi prepared Chang'e's favorite food and put it in the garden under the moonlight as a memorial ceremony for Chang'e, which became the Moon Festival.

"And that's where she lives now—on the moon, with only Jade Rabbit to keep her company," said Mama. "Because Houyi died here on Earth. Now she waits for him on the moon above."

"Forever?" asked Fei Fei.

"Forever," confirmed Mama and Baba.

When Mother told the story, the words wrapped around Fei Fei, and she felt as if she could see and feel everything that Chang'e did. The sorrow, the

loneliness, but the power of love as well. For true love, Chang'e was willing to wait forever.

Mama tossed the scarf into the air. As the scarf came down, it looked as if the image of Chang'e was swaying, floating back to the ground, thought Fei Fei. But the real Chang'e never came back to Earth, of course. Baba caught the scarf and wrapped it tenderly around Mama's shoulders.

"Do you think Chang'e is real?" Fei Fei asked Baba.

"If your mother says she's real, then she is absolutely real," said Baba with a certainty usually reserved for multiplication tables and the names of plants. His confidence comforted Fei Fei; Chang'e was definitely real if Baba said so.

"Thank you!" said Mama. Then she leaned down to Fei Fei and whispered, "Look up. Can you see Jade Rabbit? He's making a potion." Her breath tickled Fei Fei's ear.

Fei Fei looked up at the pale, dappled moon. On a clear night like this, she could just make out the rabbit's ears made up of gray spots on the moon's surface. "I can see him!" said Fei Fei. "He's making moooon mush!" This was also part of their story.

"Moooon mush!" said Baba. Mama and Fei Fei laughed when Baba said it; it sounded funnier coming from someone who usually preferred the facts. Fei Fei's and her mother's laughs were alike, with little snorting sounds.

Fei Fei ran ahead of her parents, over the bridge, feeling the wind tug at the paper lantern in her hand. "Bunny rocket comin' through! Look at my rocket ship!" She tapped the nose of the stone lion, one of a pair guarding the bridge near her house. She ran straight to their home and their family's mooncake bakery. Fei Fei loved everything about her house; she loved the bakery that extended off the first floor and the way the roof sloped down, making the house seem cozy. She loved the windows that opened outward and the pots of bamboo they grew outside and the way the house smelled sweet from making mooncakes. Mama and Baba followed, stepping carefully over the threshold. Fei Fei zoomed through the bakery, making rocket sounds.

"Slow down there, little bunny," said Mama. She picked up Fei Fei's small apron. "How about you help us make mooncakes today?" She wrapped the apron strings around Fei Fei and tied them in the back.

"I can?" Usually Fei Fei was told she was too small to help. This was a new development.

"I think it's about time you learn how we make our special family mooncakes," said Mama with a gentle laugh.

The two other bakers were already at work, making the golden, round mooncakes. Fei Fei's parents joined in. Together, their movements flowed. Stuff, roll, press, smack! The mooncakes came out of the presses. The presses made designs on each mooncake; Fei Fei used her finger to trace the raised ridges. The rhythm and energy filled the kitchen. Everyone had a job, and they carried it out just in time for the next person to take over. Their work together was as perfect and whole as a circle, like her family, and now she was part of it.

Fei Fei's mother showed her how to roll the dough and make it ready for the filling. Fei Fei's hands were small, but she was quick to learn. Her small fingers rolled and pressed the dough. Her first mooncake was perfect! Her parents beamed proudly. The family business would be in good hands for the next generation. Stuff, roll, press, smack!

Fei Fei's responsibilities grew with her as she got older. She could be counted on to make the filling, and she went with Mama into the village to sell mooncakes. She and her parents were a team.

But then their lives changed, sending Fei Fei down a path she never expected.

It started one day when Fei Fei and her mother were in the kitchen, getting ready to take a batch of mooncakes out of the oven. Mama suddenly tipped to one side, her face going pale. Baba went over to steady her.

Mama rarely got sick, but that wasn't what worried Fei Fei. Anyone could get sick. It was the look on her mother's face as she tried to regain her balance. Mama was scared, which scared Fei Fei.

"Look," said Mama. She held up the mooncakes, trying to create a distraction. Fei Fei could hear her words even before she said them. *"Cherish life and everything you love. Magic in these mooncakes for you."* By the time she was done speaking, Mama had set herself upright. But now a cold handprint settled over Fei Fei's heart, one that would stay for a long time.

Mama started to go to the doctor often after that. She still laughed but maybe not as loudly. Sometimes she needed a moment to catch her breath or gather her strength. Then, it seemed, she and Fei Fei slowly changed places. Fei Fei was the one who pushed the cart loaded with mooncakes while Mama walked slowly beside her. Fei Fei tried to take on even more work so Mama did not have to do so much. Fei Fei was the one who conducted the sales. She calculated the prices in her head. Fei Fei knew how to keep the conversation lively to keep the customers talking until they bought a box of mooncakes.

"Flaky, sweet, and delicious! Homemade mooncakes!" Fei Fei would call out as they walked down the street. "Did you know that if you put forty billion mooncakes side by side you could reach the moon?" she asked a customer who had asked for ten.

"That's a lot of mooncakes," said the man.

"'Course if the moon is at its farthest point from the Earth, you'd need four hundred twenty-six million two hundred thirty-two more!" The enormous numbers thrilled Fei Fei—the impossible became possible if you could measure it.

"You better get baking," said the man. He walked away, laughing.

"Magic in these mooncakes for you," Mama called out softly. She said the words like a promise. Then she tickled Fei Fei with a flower she had found. But even those small things seemed to deplete her energy. Mama was slipping away even as they clung to each other.

As Mama grew sicker and their lives seemed to skid and change from day to day, they still had one constant: their spot at the canal where they made so many memories. The family went back to their spot on the canal one day when the leaves were growing more brittle and the air was cold. Mama had a hard time walking. Fei Fei tried to feel happy to have a special outing. The Moon Festival, the time when they sold the most mooncakes, was coming. Mama sang one of her mooncake songs. Her voice was growing weaker. Fei Fei shivered even though she was wearing a coat. The moment felt special but in a sorrowful way.

Mama and Baba had a surprise. "Open it," they said, handing Fei Fei a box. The lid bounced open and a small white rabbit popped onto Fei Fei's lap. The rabbit peered up at her, her eyes fluttering under long lashes. Fei Fei's sad heart filled with joy.

She gasped. "I love her!" The rabbit leaped out of the box into Fei Fei's arms. Fei Fei decided to call her Bungee, because she bounced like bungee cords.

Fei Fei's parents held her in an embrace as she held Bungee. Fei Fei felt the tiny warmth from Bungee in her arms and the larger circle of protection from the wind by her parents. They were making a memory, a memory of Bungee joining their family and being together. Fei Fei tried to take it all in: the soft rabbit fur against her fingers, her father's wool coat against her cheek, her mother's rose-scented soap. Don't forget this moment, she told herself. There is magic in this moment. She didn't want it to end.

But their time together did end, taking away Mama, taking away part of Fei Fei.

The next time Fei Fei went to the river, it was with Baba and Bungee only. Mama was gone. The world became incomplete because nothing could fill the hole in Fei Fei's heart. All the colors in the world, the warmth of the sun, the sweet notes of music disappeared because her mother was not on the Earth with her. Fei Fei could not believe she was standing on the Earth without her. It did not seem physically possible. Her heart and her brain fought each other to understand. Mama is gone, said her brain. It's not possible, said her heart.

Fei Fei knelt by the river and released a lotus flower onto the currents, the delicate petals contrasting with the rough currents of the water. They watched the flower float away until it disappeared from their sight. It was another way to say goodbye, another promise to remember her mother. This is where her heart and mind agreed: they would never forget Mama. True love never forgets.

Chapter One

In the early dawn of the day, Fei Fei took a freshly baked mooncake and placed it on the household altar and let herself revel in memories of her mother for a moment—sitting by the canal, learning to make mooncakes, hearing her mother's laugh. She tried to keep those memories sharp, bright and new as a freshly polished mirror. She focused on the details. What did it feel like when Mama held her hand? What did Mama's eyes look like when she smiled? How did Mama tie her scarf?

Fei Fei wondered if her mother would recognize her now. She had gotten taller, of course. But maybe it was her hair that was the most different. When she was little, her mother had brushed her long hair for her until it hung straight and shining. Young Fei Fei would lose herself in those moments with her mother. And now, an older Fei Fei would lose herself in the memory of those moments. After her mother died, Fei Fei had cut her hair short and kept it that way, letting her hair stick out in odd places. She was a different person now. Without her mother, Fei Fei's natural long straight hair was too painful to keep.

Bungee had gotten bigger, too. The small rabbit was now full-grown, and a great companion to Fei Fei. Everyone in the village was used to seeing them together—the girl with spiky hair and her white rabbit.

Fei Fei went back to the kitchen, where she and her father rolled out mooncake dough together. Fei Fei and Baba remembered to hold the rolling pins the way Mama had taught them. Another moment, another memory, but neither of them said anything. Instead, Fei Fei leaned her head against her father's shoulder. They had each other, and that was all that mattered.

As the sun rose farther above the horizon, the

village bustled to life. Soon it was time to open the windows of the bakery. Fei Fei filled the displays with golden mooncakes and took pictures of the customers, wishing them a happy Moon Festival. "Zhongqiujie kuaile!" The Moon Festival was also known as the Mid-Autumn Festival.

"Qie zi!" Fei Fei encouraged the customers to smile as she took their photos. The camera spat out the photos, and Fei Fei added them to the board full of pictures of happy customers.

"What a team," said Baba, walking by with more boxes. He loaded up Fei Fei's bike in the driveway, and they began a familiar checklist.

"Mooncakes?" asked Fei Fei.

"Check," said Dad. "We got bungee cords?"

"Check," said Fei Fei.

"You got Bungee?" Fei Fei laughed as Bungee leaped into the front basket and found a comfy spot. This was their custom, Bungee riding with Fei Fei.

Baba helped Fei Fei adjust the gears on the bike. He checked the bike over, making sure it was safe. "All right," he said. "Hey, we've got company tonight, so don't be late, okay?"

"I'll be back in time," promised Fei Fei. Then she giggled and pointed to a smudge on Baba's face. "Baba." She indicated the spot on her own face, and Baba wiped off the oil with the back of his hand. They needed so few words to communicate.

"Careful now!" said Baba as Fei Fei sped off, nearly knocking over an unsuspecting pedestrian.

"Oh, sorry!" called Fei Fei. Bungee held on to the basket

The two began their route through the village. They went over the bridge with the two stone lions. Fei Fei patted one for luck as she pedaled out of the main part of the village. They passed a group of people doing tai chi. They came to their first stop: a canola field, the yellow flowers swaying with the wind. A group of people gathered to buy mooncakes. Fei Fei and Bungee sold some boxes, then continued through the field.

"See you next week, Fei Fei!"

From the fields Fei Fei sped to a construction site, trading the crop-filled fields for hard metal rails running across the ground. A new maglev rail was being built; soon trains would race by, relying on the push of magnets to float over the track. Fei Fei stopped to admire the progress and then got down to business.

"Scrumptious mooncakes, fresh for tonight!" Fei Fei announced.

"We'll take four," said one of the rail workers.

"Four? Why not sixteen?" Fei Fei handed over three more boxes. "You fellas must get pretty hungry building the fastest train in the world!" She gazed at the billboard behind them, which showed the sleek train that would come soon.

"You know about the maglev?" The rail worker seemed surprised that the young girl knew what they were doing, but Fei Fei was just getting started. She took the opportunity to get a closer look from the platform.

"I heard about it in school. It doesn't even bother

with wheels. It floats on electromagnetic fields, like on a cushion of air." Fei Fei was the one in class who figured out that floating meant there was no friction to slow down the train. "The magnets also help propel the trains. Whoosh! Magnetic levitation is the coolest!"

The rail workers were impressed. As Fei Fei rode away, one said, "Huh . . . did you know that's how it works?" Another one, with a mouth already full of mooncake, managed to respond, "Mmmm . . . nope."

Chapter Two

Fei Fei could not wait to get home to tell Baba that she had sold all the boxes. As soon as she got home, she jumped off the bike and ran inside the house. "Baba! I sold all the mooncakes tod—"

The sight of a bag of red dates stopped her. Some people used dates for the mooncake filling, but they never did in Fei Fei's family bakery. None of Mama's recipes used them.

"I thought we'd try something new in honor of our guest," said Baba. His voice sounded a little strange—a little too formal. "Fei Fei, this is Mrs. Zhong."

A slender woman took a step toward Fei Fei. She had warm eyes and a broad smile. She tucked her hair behind her ear. "Hi, Fei Fei." She greeted Fei Fei familiarly, as if she already knew her.

Baba had mentioned a guest, but this woman

was not who Fei Fei was expecting. "Hello," responded Fei Fei politely. She wondered why Mrs. Zhong, a stranger, would come to their house on a day for family celebrations.

"It's nice to—" Mrs. Zhong gestured with her hands and knocked a bowl of dates onto the floor. "Oh! Sorry, sorry." The woman's ears turned red. She began to clean up, and Baba bent next to her to help.

"Oh!"

"Oh no, I'm so sorry."

"Don't worry about it," said Baba soothingly. Fei Fei was not used to Baba talking like that to anyone but her. A prickle of jealousy ran down her spine. He repeated himself. "Don't worry about it."

"I can't believe I just did that," said Mrs. Zhong. Her hands were shaking as she picked up the bowl that had fallen to the floor. Father reached out to steady the bowl, and their hands touched. They seemed to pause for a moment, as if time had stopped. Fei Fei stared.

"Uh, how about a tour!" said Baba awkwardly.

He stood back up and took a small step away from Mrs. Zhong. He gave Fei Fei a look of silent apology. Mrs. Zhong was more than just a visitor. Then he spoke to Mrs. Zhong. "You haven't seen the shop."

"I'd love to," said Mrs. Zhong. As they headed into the shop, Mrs. Zhong rebuked herself one more time. "Ugh, I can't believe I did that."

Baba laughed. "That's where we make the mooncakes, and this is where we sell them. . . ." Fei Fei thought she heard him say her name, but it didn't matter. Baba was taking a stranger into their private world. Fei Fei felt ill. This woman did not belong there. Fei Fei had been looking forward to the evening celebration, but now she was not so sure.

Fei Fei felt something move over her, brushing the top of her head. Her head spun. What was happening? A boy, about four years younger than she was, appeared. "Leapfrog!" he shouted.

"What?" said Fei Fei. She forced her eyes to focus on this other new person. The boy had short bristly hair, and his ears stuck out like wings on an airplane. The only thing bigger than his ears was his mouth, which apparently was capable of making very loud noises.

The boy mistook her shocked expression for attention. He pulled out a Ping-Pong paddle from his pocket and twirled it while giving her an enormous smile.

"C'mon! Leap over me!" he urged.

"No!" Fei Fei responded, still shocked by the sudden appearance of this loud, small creature.

"What? You don't know leapfrog?" The boy pulled out something green and rubbery from his pocket. It was an actual, live frog. "Here, watch Croak."

"You can't let a frog loose in here!" Fei Fei gasped. Neither the boy nor the frog seemed to understand. Croak hopped straight toward Bungee. Fei Fei grabbed the frog just before it reached her precious rabbit and handed it back to the boy.

"Who exactly *are* you?" she asked.

"You just met my mom!" chirped the boy. "I'm Chin. I got fourth place in the Yanshi City Ping-Pong Club tournament. . . . Shoulda been third." He pointed to an emblem on his shirt. "Oh, oh, oh, and by the way, I have a superpower. Can you guess what it is?"

"Super annoying?" snapped Fei Fei. This loud-mouthed boy was more than she could bear.

Chin's eyes lit up. "I have two superpowers! Look over there. What do you see?"

"A wall," said Fei Fei.

"To you, it's a wall," bragged Chin. "To me, it's just something to run through."

"You can run through walls?" Fei Fei asked, her tone clearly suggesting that she was not at all convinced.

"Wanna see?" Chin's eyes widened with excitement.

"Why yes," she said drily. "I'd love to."

Chin carefully set his Ping-Pong paddle on the table and then assumed a warrior stance, spreading his legs wide. Then he let out a scream. "No barriers! Raaaah!" He lowered his head like a charging bull and ran straight into the wall. He hit it so hard that the stone shook and a towel fell from the clothesline. But the wall remained.

A Ping-Pong ball slowly dribbled toward Fei Fei as Chin wobbled to his feet. To her surprise, Chin was not discouraged. In fact, he seemed rather triumphant.

"Did you see that? Almost a whole part of me went through that wall. My molecules opened up."

Utter nonsense, thought Fei Fei. The evening had not even begun, and already it seemed too much. She picked up Bungee and began to walk out of the bakery. Chin called to her retreating back. "I could feel the molecules separate. It's like the universe was calling me by name!"

Fei Fei could not get the annoying boy out of her thoughts. As she helped Baba hang up lanterns in the courtyard, she tried to explain to him why the boy was so annoying.

"Baba, he ran into a wall!" The words did not seem to do an adequate job of showing how stupid the activity was.

"Aha! Eight-year-old boys have a lot of energy. Give him a pass this time," said Baba kindly.

"'This time'?" exclaimed Fei Fei. She had been counting the minutes until this horrible evening might end and she would never ever have to see Mrs. Zhong or Chin again. The thought of *another* time was almost more than she could bear.

"His mother is, um, very nice. Yeah? I think you should talk to her." Instead of his usual confident tone, Baba's words were tripping over themselves like the feet of a person trying to walk in shoes that are too big.

"Why?" asked Fei Fei.

Baba turned to look at her. His face was very gentle. "Once you get to know her, I think you'll like her. It's good to meet new people," he said.

"Yeah . . . but why?" she asked. "I have you; we have each other." She watched as Baba took a light bulb out of a lantern to test it. The bulb jingled lightly, signaling that it was broken.

"Um, of course, sweetheart. We're always going to have each other. . . ." Baba stopped to get a new light bulb. He handed it to her, and she screwed it in. The lantern glowed to life.

Baba knelt down. "Fei Fei, there is something important I've been wanting to talk to you about. You know how since, uh . . ." She and her father had had many discussions, but this one was different. It made her feel nervous. But before they could finish talking, the rest of the family arrived. Fei Fei's grandfather, grandmother, and two aunts and an uncle bustled in, talking over each other. Happy noises that Fei Fei recognized. She ran to greet her family, feeling relieved.

"Hello! Anybody order twelve big hairy crabs?" asked Auntie Ling.

"Oh yeah, my favorite!" said Fei Fei. The sights of familiar family and food cheered her. The family got to work in the kitchen. Soon the stove was full of bubbling pots and pans. The aunties were in charge of the large wok, dumping in vegetables that sizzled as soon as they hit the hot oil.

"That sizzle!" said Auntie Ling.

"These dumplings, almost as good as mine," said Grandma. She beckoned Fei Fei to her and then popped a dumpling into her mouth. "You're so skinny; hasn't anybody been feeding you?" she asked Fei Fei.

"Coming through!" sang Auntie Mei.

Grandpa followed her. "The hairy crab is a burrowing crab, known for its furry claws," he announced to anyone who would listen.

Fei Fei took a tray of bowls and dishes outside. Mrs. Zhong approached her, holding a towel full of red dates.

"Fei Fei, perhaps we can use my red dates for a batch of mooncakes?" Mrs. Zhong asked hopefully.

Fei Fei looked at her shiftily. "Mama preferred melon seeds in the paste," she said.

Mrs. Zhong was unfazed by Fei Fei's quip. "Oh

well, my family uses dates grown in our garden. If you want to try one, they're delicious."

"I'm probably allergic to dates." Fei Fei lifted her chin. "Besides, we only make them our special way here." She was careful to say "our" in a way so that Mrs. Zhong knew it didn't include her. Then Fei Fei walked away.

Baba and Uncle carried a table out to the patio, and the aunties put a cloth over it and then put a lazy Susan in the middle. Then they began to fill the circular tray with food. A whole fish, to signify prosperity. Dumplings shaped like the gold ingots of China long ago. Spring rolls to attract good fortune. Round balls of sticky rice to symbolize completeness and family togetherness. Long noodles for long life and happiness. Fei Fei helped set the table. Bungee hopped into one of the chairs.

"No rabbits at the table," Fei Fei reminded her. "Besides, that's my chair." Bungee sadly hopped off the chair.

Baba and Mrs. Zhong approached the table and

admired the bounty of food. "Oh, the table looks beautiful. Where should I sit?" asked Mrs. Zhong.

Fei Fei watched in horror as her father pulled out the chair that Bungee had just abandoned. That was Fei Fei's chair. Worse still, Baba seemed completely unaware that he was doing anything wrong. He and Mrs. Zhong were too busy giggling. "Come sit by me," he said to Mrs. Zhong. Which didn't seem that funny at all.

"The hairy crab invades local waters, damaging fishing nets and native species," declared Grandpa to no one in particular. The family arranged themselves around the table and began to enjoy the dinner. Fei Fei sat far from her usual seat, but no one noticed. Tendrils of steam arose from the dishes into the cool night air. Grandma looked up.

"Oh, look how big and bright that moon is!" she exclaimed.

Fei Fei was too distracted by Mrs. Zhong and her father to look at the beautiful moon. They seemed to be in their own little world. "You have a little bit of, uh, sauce on the side of your . . ." Mrs. Zhong pointed. She and Baba laughed together.

"It's gonna be *huge* for the Moon Festival!" said Grandma, who did not notice the giggling.

"Mom's favorite holiday," said Fei Fei. That got Baba's attention. He stopped giggling and glanced away, taking a long sip of his drink. But Mrs. Zhong met her eyes.

"So, your father tells me you're fond of Chang'e," she said.

Fei Fei glared at her father. That information was private. The aunties joined the conversation.

"Ugh, poor lady that goddess! So lonely up there on the moon," said Auntie Mei. "No one but Jade Rabbit to keep her company." *Crack!* Grandpa cracked open his first of many hairy crabs. His plate was piled high with them.

Auntie Ling made an impatient sound. "Oh, come on! Chang'e loves it up there alone. She didn't need to gobble both pills to keep them from Feng Meng. She took both immortality pills instead of saving one for Houyi so she'd be by herself!"

"Houyi the Archer!" yelped Chin. He positioned his arms as if he were drawing the string of a bow, which Fei Fei thought was rude and quite bad enough. Did no one teach this boy any table manners? But then it got worse. He launched Croak like an arrow high across the table. Onto Fei Fei's head. The frog landed in her hair with a wet *thwack*.

"Chin!" Mrs. Zhong gasped.

"Augh!" grunted Fei Fei. She removed the frog from her head and handed it to her uncle, trying to touch as little of it as possible. She might have given Chin a glare, but she was intent on correcting the story of Chang'e. She did not like the version of the story where Chang'e had behaved selfishly by taking the potion or both pills for herself.

"That's not what happened, Auntie! Houyi was fighting off demons—"

"With his bow and arrow!" interrupted Chin.

Fei Fei raised her voice to drown out the boy. "WHEN Feng Meng came and tried to ste—"

Auntie Ling wouldn't let her finish. "Steal the immortality pills. Yeah, yeah, yeah, she only put them both in her mouth as a hiding place. Not buying it."

Auntie Mei joined in. "Chang'e floated to the sky while her one true love stayed here." She sighed and looked dreamily toward the sky.

"And bit the dust." Auntie Ling was less romantic than Auntie Mei.

"Now she lives with a rabbit instead of a husband," pointed out Uncle.

"Good choice," said Auntie Ling. She spun the lazy Susan, trying to get to the crabs again.

"But it wasn't her choice!" cried Fei Fei. "She didn't try to leave Houyi behind. She misses Houyi and cries for him every day!"

"How do you know that?" asked Auntie Ling.

"They text," joked Grandpa.

"Don't tease Fei Fei," admonished Auntie Mei.

"It's just a silly myth," said Auntie Ling. The crabs had almost reached her.

Fei Fei put her own hands on the lazy Susan. "It's not a silly myth. It's real. Chang'e is real." She swung back on the tray, hard, causing all the crabs to spill onto the table. The beautiful table of food was ruined.

"Fei Fei," said Baba, reprimanding her lightly.

She stepped away from the table and turned her face toward the night sky. "She's on the moon right now!" she cried. "Waiting for her one and only true love. Waiting . . ."

The family stared at Fei Fei in disbelief. She turned to her father for support. "Right, Baba?" The words "one and only true love" still hung in the air.

Baba looked at Mrs. Zhong, his face reddening. "Uh . . ." He seemed unsure what the correct answer was.

Grandma tried to change the subject. "Everyone, the food is getting cold. Let's eat."

Fei Fei stared at the ground. They all seemed embarrassed for her, but they were the ones who were mistaken. They were the ones who should feel foolish, not her! She started to run out of the courtyard. Mrs. Zhong leaned over to reach her, but Fei Fei was just out of her grasp. She saw Baba make a motion to get up, but Grandma stopped him. "Let her cool off," she said.

As Fei Fei ran into the house, she overheard Auntie Ling say, "She's at the top of her class, but she still believes in Chang'e?"

Of course I believe in Chang'e, thought Fei Fei. To believe in Chang'e was to believe in the power of true love. And who didn't believe in true love?

She was afraid she might know the answer. She replayed her father's expression in her mind when she asked him to confirm Chang'e's existence. His face had turned blank, then embarrassed. How could he not believe in Chang'e? When did he stop believing?

Fei Fei rushed over to Bungee's basket, picked up the bunny, and held her against her heart. The rabbit's warm softness comforted her.

"It's you and me, Bungee. We're the last of the true believers," said Fei Fei. Bungee stared back at her with big eyes. Fei Fei embraced Bungee again, burying her face in her delicate fur.

Then *dink!* Something hit Fei Fei on the head. "Ah!" she exclaimed, setting Bungee back down. Then it happened again. "Ow!" She looked up to see Chin sitting in the rafters. He was bouncing a Ping-Pong ball with his paddle. He popped another one at her.

"Ugh, not really in the mood," said Fei Fei through gritted teeth. She was trying to regain her composure, but it wasn't easy with someone so constantly irritating.

Chin flipped over so he hung by his knees from the rafters. "Know what I am?" he asked. "A BAT!" He spread his arms wide and wiggled them.

"Yeah, a *ding*bat," retorted Fei Fei.

"Well, I hope you like dingbats! Because you're going to see a whole lot more of me!" The boy fell off the rafters and landed on the ground with a clumsy thud. He groaned and then got to his feet.

"Not if I can help it," she said.

"Haven't you heard?" asked Chin. "We're going to be brother and sister!"

He said the words with genuine delight. But Fei Fei felt nothing but horror.

"What?" she asked, hoping she had misunderstood.

"My mom and your dad are getting mar—"

She wouldn't let him finish. "Don't say it! Don't!" She turned to go up the stairs, but Mrs. Zhong appeared.

"Hi, Fei Fei," she said. Then she extended her hand. "I didn't want you to miss dessert. I saved you a special mooncake from my hometown . . . without dates." She handed Fei Fei a small tin box.

Fei Fei struggled to receive the gift politely. It took all of her self-control not to scream. "Thank you," she managed.

Chin ran past them toward the kitchen. "No barriers!" he yelled. The next sound they heard was a crash, then the *tap-tap-tap* of a loose Ping-Pong ball bouncing out of the kitchen.

"Oh, Chin can be rambunctious at times. But after a while you get used to him," said Mrs. Zhong to Fei Fei. She looked after her son with a mixture of fondness and weariness.

"Get over here so I can kick everyone's butt at mahjong!" called Auntie Mei to Mrs. Zhong. Fei Fei could already hear the sounds of tiles spilling and clicking across the table.

Mrs. Zhong's face brightened. "Oh ho! Yes! We'll see!" she called back. She walked back to rejoin the merry group while Fei Fei fled upstairs, finally free of the burdens of trying to be well behaved. She rushed into her bedroom and slammed the door behind her.

"'Get used to him'?" she repeated to herself. "I'll never get used to him! What's so 'special' about your mooncake?" She tossed the tin box into a desk drawer. "I don't want it, and I don't want *you*."

She flung herself onto her bed and held her

Chang'e doll close to her. "I just want things back the way they were," she said desperately. Her eyes filled with tears. "He used to believe in Chang'e! He said she was absolutely real! But now he's changed. If Baba could only believe again, he would never marry that woman. H-he would remember everything."

Fei Fei took her mother's scarf off the bedpost where she kept it and buried her face into the silky cloth, trying to find the scent of her mother's rose soap. It was growing fainter. "He would remember you," she whispered. She looked toward the window, where a slice of moonbeam cut in, filling the room with a bluish glow.

Bungee slowly hopped toward the window, her fur radiating with moonlight. Then, with one swift motion, she jumped over the sill and disappeared into the night.

Chapter Three

"Bungee!" Fei Fei raced out of the house and began running up and down the street. Her heart thudded in her chest as her eyes searched. She could not bear the thought of losing Bungee. Bungee was so small, and the village was so big, at least in comparison. She breathed a sigh of relief when she found the rabbit tucked under some leaves. Bungee led her toward the river. A tall, elegant crane perched nearby but took flight in one motion as she approached.

My name means "fly," thought Fei Fei. But I never will. Not like that.

Bungee had led her to the spot by that canal that held so many memories, where Fei Fei had laughed about Space Dog and her parents had given her Bungee. Where she had set the lotus flower on the water and watched it float away. She knelt at the edge of the dock, trying to take it all in.

"Mama," she whispered. "Why is this happening?" The cold night gave her no answers.

Fei Fei hugged herself and pretended it was her mother's embrace. She shut her eyes and imagined her mother's face, full of life and light. Her stories of Chang'e and stardust. When Chang'e floated up to heaven, she left her true love, Houyi, behind. The stories, the laughter, the circle they made together, that was true love, too. Her mother's love was still real, as real as anything she could touch on Earth. Why had Baba forgotten Mama and the love they had? Why did he deny that Chang'e existed when he used to say that she was absolutely real? Fei Fei's chest ached as her heart and mind clashed. Chang'e was waiting for Houyi because their love was eternal. Why couldn't Baba wait?

Fei Fei gently pushed a lotus flower into the water, wishing she could float away like the flower and escape her problems. How could she prove that Chang'e was real when she was hundreds of thousands of kilometers, hundreds of millions of mooncakes, away.

She heard the rush of wings and turned her head just in time to see a crane fly in front of the moon, creating a beautiful black silhouette in the white circle. The bird and the moon were one. In that moment, the light from the moon seemed to shine only upon Fei Fei. There was a solution to her problems, she realized.

A breeze swept over her, lifting up her hair and giving her goose bumps. She went back to the house and hopped on her bike, as if her thoughts were moving too quickly for her to stand still. She rode her bike around the town, over the bridge, and then to the tallest pagoda. She ran up the stairs to the peak. It was as close to the moon as she could get. But she could get closer, couldn't she?

What if she built a rocket? What if she could fly to the moon to see Chang'e and bring back proof to her father that Chang'e—and Baba's love for Fei

Fei's mother—really existed? If she could bring back a photo to prove that Chang'e really existed, her father would not marry Mrs. Zhong. He would wait. She was a smart girl; she was first in her class! Maybe she could make it happen.

For the next few days, Fei Fei immersed herself in rockets. She watched videos of rockets being launched into space and found diagrams of rockets. She filled the walls of her room with equations and then tore them down. Everything she had ever learned in science was helping her now. She had always been an excellent student, but this task took every bit of her abilities. To keep herself motivated, she drew a picture of herself and added it to her Chang'e poster. This is what's going to happen, she told herself. This is what our selfie is going to look like.

Fei Fei learned that her ancestors had invented black gunpowder and then invented fire arrows propelled by that gunpowder, which allowed the arrows to travel farther and more powerfully than before. These were really the earliest kinds of rockets. Maybe her ancestors had launched fire arrows into the sky. Maybe rocket building was in her blood.

Thrust. Escape velocity. Nozzles. Propellant. Payload. Fei Fei taught herself as much about rockets as she could, until the terms and concepts seemed to be part of her. Nose cone. Fin. Combustion chamber. She calculated the weight a rocket could carry; the more weight the rocket had, the more power she needed, so Fei Fei tried to pare down what was in the rocket.

All she needed now were the supplies.

"Baba, can I borrow the credit card for this science project I'm working on?" she asked one day in the kitchen. Fei Fei was careful to look only at her father and not Mrs. Zhong or Chin, who were also there. It seemed like they were always there, getting in the way, trying to look over her shoulder. Fei Fei tried to temper the pinpricks of annoyance she felt by reminding herself that after she came back from the moon with the photo, they would have to go. When she came back from the moon, things would go back to the way they were.

"Um . . . sure," said Baba uncertainly. He did not seem sure how to talk to Fei Fei these days. He handed her the card. Chin leaned over to see her plans, but she pulled them away before he could get a look. Fei Fei began placing her orders on her computer, clicking as fast as her fingers would allow. Space helmet. Rocket boots. Pumps. Valves. Windows. An assortment of oddly shaped packages soon followed. Fei Fei carried them away as quickly as they arrived, keeping her quest a secret.

Explosions, she told herself, are part of the road to success. Then she yawned and tried to pay attention in class.

She had expected that building a rocket would be difficult, but still, the explosions were disheartening. Several rockets had blown up, sometimes so forcefully that the explosions knocked her over. One rocket did manage to launch before it came back to Earth and exploded. And then knocked her over.

It was hard to concentrate on what the teacher was talking about, so Fei Fei took out a sheet of paper and began working on a new design. Maybe if she could make the opening of the nozzle a little larger, but would she sacrifice acceleration? The problem was that the rocket needed to achieve escape velocity—the speed and power necessary to push past the gravitational pull of the Earth. Gravity was the reason that the rockets kept coming back.

The teacher loomed at the front of the class. "Something you want to share with us?" he asked Fei Fei loudly. The whole class stopped and stared at her. She had been caught. She knew what came next, though she used to be the kind of student who was never scolded, only praised.

Fei Fei walked slowly to the front of the classroom and held out the picture. The teacher snatched it away. She hung her head in shame.

"Today you are number one in class. But maybe tomorrow you'll be number thirty," said the teacher sternly. "There's no doodling allowed in class." He stuck the picture to the wall, being sure to stick the tack in the middle of the picture.

Some of the students snickered at the contrast between Fei Fei's roughly drawn rocket and the poster next to it, a stylish rendering of the maglev. But Fei Fei saw something different. The picture had swiveled around the tack so that the rocket was in line with the train. Her face broke into a huge smile. Her moment of shame had turned to triumph. Her problem was solved. The maglev would help get her to the moon.

With a clear solution in her mind, Fei Fei mapped out her design on graph paper for the rocket. *The* rocket. Her rocket. She needed more materials. An old washing machine door. Scraps from other rockets. A seat belt. Her hope grew with the rocket, expanding beyond her wildest dreams. This one

would work. This was the rocket that would take her to the moon. "Power, lift, duration, gyro navigation," she chanted to herself as she worked, as if giving those powers to the rocket. To keep the rocket safe from prying eyes, she carefully designed a costume for it. When it was time to take the rocket to the maglev, Fei Fei towed the rocket hidden in a large paper rabbit behind her bike.

The townspeople were used to seeing a bunny in the front of the bicycle, so a large rabbit trailing behind wasn't that strange.

At the track, Fei Fei unloaded the rabbit from her bike and attached the magnets. A maglev train achieves great speeds because it uses magnets to levitate the train off the ground and then another set of magnets to propel the train forward. She carefully placed the magnets on the edges of the rocket and another set under the track. She was so close. Fei Fei hurried back home to get the last of her things. Her Chang'e doll. A camera, for proof. What else does a person need on the moon, anyway? She kept most of what she needed in her desk, didn't she? Impulsively, she swept the contents of her desk drawer into her backpack. They didn't weigh that much, she told herself. She'd still be okay.

Finally, it was time. The night air was cool, but there was not too much wind. Good conditions for flight. Fei Fei tore the papier-mâché away from the rocket window so she would be able to see outside. The moon hung brightly in the dark sky, like a welcome sign. Then she climbed inside the rocket, buckled Bungee into her seat, and carefully put the helmet on her own head. Her heart was pounding. She'd never been so close.

This is it, she thought. Soon she would be on the moon, meeting Chang'e. Gravity would not hold her down.

"Chang'e," she whispered. "I am coming to you."

She set a photo of herself, Mama, and Baba on the dashboard. She touched the photo tenderly. All of this, all of this effort and sacrifice, was for love so evident in the photo. Then she flicked a few switches and felt the engine roar to life. Her seat was rumbling. There was just one more step. She leaned forward and pressed the Launch button.

Chapter Four

The rocket rolled lazily backward and then, bit by bit, began to move forward, down the track. The rocket moved so slowly, Fei Fei swore she could see a snail outside moving faster. Bungee lurched in her seat, trying to make the rocket go faster.

The rocket, Fei Fei knew, needed to move much faster to escape gravity. She looked at the speedometer. The numbers ticked up, bit by tiny bit, as the rocket made its way down the track, but not fast enough. Fei Fei had no other plan. If this didn't work, she didn't know what she would do next.

Then a hum came on. The magnets were kicking in. The numbers began to roll faster. The rocket accelerated smoothly, lightly. 9 . . . 21 . . . 25 . . . 29 . . .

The spaceship was now hurtling down the

track. Faster, faster, faster! *Whoosh!* The view outside the window was becoming a blur. The rocket filled with a loud, churning *thud.* 266 . . . 297 . . . 356 . . . Fei Fei felt a force against her body pushing her into the seat.

She allowed herself a small smile and then hit another button. Wings shot out from the sides, and the rabbit costume slid off, revealing the full-blown rocket. Fei Fei's amazing, beautiful, powerful rocket.

487 . . . 502 . . . 623 . . .

The rocket lifted away from the track and curved into the sky. Fei Fei hit one more button, and fireworks exploded from the back in a gorgeous bouquet of firepower, providing the last bit of extra propulsion they needed. She watched from her tablet. The Earth was racing away, growing tinier by the second.

Fei Fei tilted her head back and laughed. "I did it! I did it!" she rejoiced. For the first time in a long time, she felt light, not weighed down by worries. Bungee also celebrated from her seat, doing her

own rabbit dance of joy. They were on their way! They were going to the moon!

But then the rocket seemed to slow its ascent, as if moving through some invisible goo. Its delightful speed disappeared. Then the rocket stopped altogether. The rocket let out one last small explosion from the back, but they were in a stall. It was as if someone had pressed Pause. Fei Fei held her breath as she frantically tried to think of a solution.

Then the rocket seemed to drop out from under her.

They were plunging back down to Earth. The rocket twirled unsteadily, like a top getting ready to tip over, making Fei Fei's head spin. She had no point of reference, no place that was the bottom or the top. Then an ear-piercing scream cut through the air, but not from Fei Fei. Not from Bungee.

It was a person. In a helmet. "We're gonna die!" the figure screamed.

The voice was oddly familiar. And annoying. "Chin?" exclaimed Fei Fei. She could make out his toothy smile from under the helmet.

"Hi, Fei Fei!" said Chin, who could not help being friendly, it seemed, even in moments of mortal danger.

"You dingbat!" screamed Fei Fei. "I didn't calculate your extra weight!" Now they were both screaming. Screaming and still falling back toward Earth.

This is it, thought Fei Fei. There was nothing they could do.

Suddenly, a bright white beam shot out of the sky and caught the plummeting spaceship. The rocket stopped falling, suspended

"Are we dead?" asked Chin. "Wha-what's happening?"

The beam of moonlight was a tractor beam, pulling the spaceship back. It felt sort of like an escalator ride, if escalators could carry rockets. Fei Fei and Chin peered out the window. Space had its own strange beauty, in its infinite darkness and millions of stars. The Earth passed below them.

But then something attacked Fei Fei's face with a weird sucking sound. She shrieked and tried to pry it off. She felt the weird, smooth surface of what had to be alien skin. Aliens. Aliens!

Or not. It was Croak, ribbiting happily.

"Chin?" Fei Fei looked for him to take responsibility for his frog.

Chin was floating around the spaceship. "Zero gravity, man!" he exclaimed. "Hey, are those diapers?" He pushed off one side of the spaceship, enjoying weightlessness. He pretended to swim.

Fei Fei reached up and grabbed on to him. "Get down here! This is no time to mess around!" she scolded him. But then she found herself grinning with delight. She had been working so hard on getting to the moon, she had neglected to think about what the journey itself would be like—to be weightless, to see the stars glowing brightly, to see the milky light of the moon grow closer. It was much more beautiful than she could have imagined. For a moment, she just allowed herself to enjoy. The moon loomed closer.

A hollow clanging sound came from outside

the ship, followed by an abrupt jolt in the previously smooth ride. Fei Fei and Chin peered up into the observation dome to see two lion faces looking back at them. Wings fanned out behind them. The two young winged lions were flying with the rocket ship, which was fine until they began to bat the spaceship around like a toy. Fei Fei, Chin, and Bungee rolled around inside the ship as the lions continued their game. Cat and mouse. Lion and rocket ship.

Then the rocket began to spin end over end. One lion had struck it too hard, sending it out of the tractor beam. The lions raced after the rocket, trying to regain control but only managing to push it farther away. The wondrous ride turned into a roller coaster of terror. Fei Fei saw the surface of the moon begin to rush toward them through the window, the small craters suddenly becoming large ones.

Fei Fei instinctively threw herself over Chin and Bungee. "Brace!" was the last thing she remembered screaming before the crash.

Chapter Five

The rocket somersaulted down a ridge and then broke open, like an egg cracking in half. Fei Fei, Chin, Bungee, and Croak spilled out, unconscious. The twin lions went to them and breathed blue mist on their faces. The group came to, now able to breathe in the moon's atmosphere. The lions picked the group up gently with their paws and began soaring over the lunar landscape, from the white gleam of one side of the moon to the cold, dark side. Fei Fei's feet dangled below her as they flew, reminding her of a roller coaster she had once ridden but so much more scary and unpredictable. She shivered as the temperature dropped, and she held Bungee more tightly to her. Then she gasped.

What looked like a tiny golden glow in the dark slowly began to grow, expanding upward and to the sides. As they drew nearer, Fei Fei could make out a dozen, brilliant neon colors surrounding the golden glow, which had turned into a tower of brilliant light. It was a city, looking like a basket of shining, glowing jewels. She read a sign: Lunaria.

"Bungee," she asked the rabbit. "Are they taking us to Chang'e?"

She watched the city turn beneath them, showing off the many buildings of all sizes, shapes, and colors. The lions threaded their way among the buildings, heading toward the tallest building, which had a moon at its topmost point. From the peak, the lions suddenly zoomed down to a platform. Once they landed, the lions released them. Chin fell to the ground while Fei Fei received a wet, sloppy kiss from one of the lions.

The building before them was nothing like Fei Fei had ever seen. It towered over them with magnificent spires. The doors opened, and the largest mooncake that Fei Fei had ever seen rolled up to them. It had a face and seemed to move under its own power.

Pah! The mooncake immediately split into three smaller mooncakes with arms and legs and faces. Each one was a different color: blue, pink, and yellow. They were the Lunettes.

"Welcome!" they said. "Hurry, come on! She's expecting you."

Fei Fei and Chin followed the Lunettes into the completely dark entryway. Fei Fei listened to the sounds of their feet tapping along the floor. Where were they going?

They entered a room, but the edges were shrouded in darkness. A faint sound began to grow in the center, accompanied by a sparkling light glowing and floating in front of Fei Fei and Chin. A figure began to flutter before them, a woman, shimmering in the sparkling light.

"Chang'e?" whispered Fei Fei, hardly daring to believe her luck.

"Ultraluminary," the woman whispered back. She shot up into the air in a column of light, then raised her hands. Glowing lights rose around Fei

Fei and Chin. It had to be Chang'e. Who else could be so beautiful, so powerful, so talented? Chang'e swept her hands downward, and a set of curtains fell at the same time, revealing a massive crowd of Lunarians, the inhabitants of the moon—odd, squishy creatures of all sizes and colors. They all looked adoringly in the direction of Chang'e.

Chang'e posed behind a sheer, glittery curtain. When she snapped her fingers, the curtains parted, and she began to sing. It was singing but not just any singing. It was the most joyous and beautiful singing that Fei Fei had ever heard. The sound poured out as pure as light and commanded Fei Fei to dance. Up in one corner, she spied a green rabbit expertly managing a sound board. His head bobbed in time to the music. That had to be Jade Rabbit, known for being clever and inventive. Bungee was also noticing Jade Rabbit.

Chang'e sang of sorrow and joy, her story of loss and then triumph. Her song was the story of arriving on the moon when it was barren, and how

Jade Rabbit helped turn it into a city of light. "I rise," she sang to a driving pop beat that matched her bright tone. "I rise!" Chang'e was clearly a diva, and this was her song.

Chin, Croak, and Bungee also began to dance; the music was too contagious not to. It thumped through their bones and propelled their feet. The whole crowd was dancing, to be part of Chang'e, to be part of her story.

But the dancing wasn't enough, not for Fei Fei. She couldn't control her excitement any longer. She found herself running toward the goddess. Fireworks exploded behind Chang'e as she struck her final pose. The crowd roared in approval . . . then stopped and gasped as a skinny girl with choppy black hair threw herself at the feet of the goddess, hugging her legs.

Chapter Six

"Oh, no she didn't!" said one of the Lunettes. "She definitely can't do that," agreed another.

Fei Fei did not care. She did not care about the disapproving looks or the raised eyebrows. Chang'e was here. Right here. Fei Fei's mission was nearly complete.

"You're . . . real," gasped Fei Fei. "And I'm so happy! And I feel so . . ." She struggled to find the right words. After so much struggle, so much pain, everything was falling into place. And Chang'e was here, ready to change Fei Fei's fate. Chang'e must have sent the lions to bring them here, Fei Fei reasoned, to meet her.

Chang'e was even more beautiful close-up. Her eyelashes fanned out from her face like butterflies. Her hair reminded Fei Fei of a bolt of lustrous, black silk. Her lips, as pink as plum blossoms, arranged themselves into a pout.

Chang'e bent down to look more closely at her. The pout turned to a frown. "Huh . . . What butcher cut your hair?" said Chang'e without even a proper greeting.

But Fei Fei was too entranced by her and the magical surroundings to be offended. I'm on the moon! she wanted to shout. I'm meeting Chang'e!

Fei Fei reached up to feel her hair, but Chang'e was not done with her inspection of the girl. "You have a round face; you need length," she said. "And you have a rogue eyebrow hair right . . . there." Without warning, a Lunette whipped out a pair of tweezers and plucked the offending hair.

"Ow!" screeched Fei Fei. Her eyebrow stung from the sudden attack.

"Improved," noted Chang'e, though she still seemed dissatisfied.

"So much better!" chimed in another Lunette.

Chang'e extended her hands, and without a

word, the Lunettes began to give her a manicure. Chang'e sighed, as if waiting for Fei Fei to be similarly aware of her unspoken wishes.

"All right, Unfortunate Hair Girl," said Chang'e. "Consider yourself welcomed. You may now give me the gift."

"Uh . . . I'm sorry?" asked Fei Fei. She had not expected this. Her mother's stories had never mentioned a gift.

Chang'e gestured impatiently with her slender hands. "My gift! You can bestow it upon me now."

Fei Fei felt her face turn to flame. "Uh . . . this is . . . awkward," she stammered. Of course, it was always proper for a guest to bring a gift to a host. In all her preparations, Fei Fei had forgotten this detail.

"Oh?" asked Chang'e. Fei Fei saw the goddess's face begin to go back to a pout.

"I wish I had a gift for you. I should have brought you something. You see, I'm in an urgent situation," explained Fei Fei.

Chang'e turned to the Lunettes. "She's talking. But it's not about the gift," she complained.

"No, Goddess," agreed Blue Lunette, the largest of the three and their apparent leader.

The gift, Fei Fei gathered from their chatter, was no ordinary gift. It was a gift needed for Houyi to return. No wonder Chang'e was so intent on getting it.

Gift or not, though, Fei Fei needed to keep going. She too had important business.

"What I mean is, you're the one who believes that love never dies! Everybody knows that about you," she said stoutly, trying to direct the conversation away from the missing gift. A little flattery also never hurt when dealing with a moody goddess.

For a moment, the goddess's expression changed. Her face softened, as if lost in a beautiful memory. Then her face snapped back. Hard. Fei Fei decided to keep talking, hoping that something she said would draw the goddess's sympathy.

"My dad used to believe that, too," said Fei Fei. She drew a deep breath and chose her words carefully. This is why she had come; she needed Chang'e to grant her request or everything she had done was in vain. "But now I'm afraid he's giving up. You have the power to change that." Now was the time to ask for her favor. It was not much to ask. "If I could just prove that you're real, just a photo, even, then he'd change his mind and—"

"Pictures. She wants pictures. Everybody wants pictures!" said Chang'e to no one in particular. She turned to Fei Fei. "Does this look like a photo op to you?" The goddess struck a pose and, impossibly, looked even more stunning than before.

"Um . . . yes?" said Fei Fei timidly.

"Then do it fast," said Chang'e. Her tone suggested that she was in a fickle mood, apt to change her mind at any moment. Fei Fei hurried to snap the photo. Click! A photo slid out of the camera. Fei Fei held her breath. Would it work?

Fei Fei watched as the photo went from black

to fuzzy green images to a very clear picture of Chang'e. She had it! She had the proof to show Baba. "Thank you. . . . Wow," said Fei Fei.

"You may now give me the gift," persisted Chang'e.

Fei Fei thought the matter of the gift had passed. Clearly, she was not the one who was supposed to bring such an important item. She fumbled. "I'm sorry, but I . . ." Her voice trailed off.

"No gift. No photo," announced Chang'e. One of the Lunettes plucked the photo from Fei Fei's hands. Fei Fei grasped at the empty air.

"You can have anything of mine that you want," said Fei Fei desperately. Her mind ran through all the possibilities of what she could offer, but really, she had nothing. There was nothing she had that would bring back Houyi. "B-b-but I don't have . . ." She was trying not to cry.

"I don't want 'anything'!" roared the goddess. "I want THE GIFT!"

This announcement was perfectly timed with Croak leaping out of Chin's pocket and landing on

Chang'e's face. Her expression turned from surprise, to horror, then fury as she realized what had just transpired. Chin tried not to giggle. Fei Fei was furious. The last thing she needed now was complications from Chin and his stupid frog!

The Lunettes looked on warily. Clearly, Chang'e's mood was souring rapidly, like a storm taking over a summer day. Chang'e peeled the frog off her face, dropped Croak unceremoniously to the ground, and glared at Fei Fei.

"I can be a little moody sometimes. Did I say sometimes? Because I meant all the time," hissed Chang'e. "Like right now, in fact. I'm feeling furious! Wild! Cranky! Listen up, Unfortunate Hair Girl. Clearly you have lost my gift. It's on the moon somewhere. And I suggest you get out there and find it!" Now she was yelling, full-throated screaming. Her eyes were wild with anger. She was nothing like the goddess Fei Fei's mother had described. Fei Fei had expected a quiet and kind goddess; this one was a volcano given to dangerous eruptions.

"But I don't know what *it* is!" pleaded Fei Fei. She was a girl who had managed to figure out many things—how to live without her mother, how to run a mooncake business, and how to get herself to the moon. But this puzzle overwhelmed her. Where would she even start?

"Of course you do!" Chang'e said. "Why else would I have sent my lions to bring you here from Earth? Let's stop playing games. We're almost out of time." She held out her hand, and a hologram of a moon appeared, hovering over her palm. Dust was falling out of the bottom of the moon, leaving just a sliver behind.

Chang'e turned to the Lunarians, who had been watching the whole time. "Lunarians! I announce a competition," said Chang'e. "Anyone who finds and brings me the gift will get a wish granted."

Chang'e turned back to Fei Fei. "If *you* bring it to me first, you'll get your photo," she told her. Then she raised her voice for the whole crowd. "Good luck and Godspeed! Find it!"

Chang'e turned to Jade Rabbit, who had quietly appeared by her side, and reminded him that she also needed the potion. The gift would not work without the potion; both were needed to bring Houyi back. Jade Rabbit nodded, aware of the importance of his task.

The audience needed no more urging from their adored queen. They all began to run, thundering out of the palace. The crowd swept up Fei Fei toward the palace exit. Chin, Croak, and Bungee followed behind.

Confusion filled the air outside the palace. Lunarians were jockeying for space, for vehicles, for an idea. "Let me through, please!" begged Fei Fei, though no one listened. Everyone was too busy thinking of what wish they would have granted by Chang'e.

Chin, though, was listening. "Wait up!" he called to Fei Fei.

She ran up to a Lunarian getting into a spaceship. "Hey! Um, can I get a—" before she could finish her sentence, the ship zoomed off. No one was going to help her.

Some more Lunarians bustled by. "Outta the way!" one barked at Fei Fei.

"A gift," said Fei Fei, forcing herself to stop and think. If she couldn't beat the Lunarians at speed, she could at least try to outthink them. A gift was something that someone gave you. For Fei Fei, that would have to be at the crash site. "What could it be?" she wondered.

Chin bounded up to her and stuck Croak in her face. "We'll help you find it!" said Chin, full of enthusiasm.

"I don't want your help!" snapped Fei Fei, remembering that Croak had accelerated Chang'e's bad mood. Chin couldn't possibly help; he'd only make things worse.

Chin wouldn't move out of the way. "First we find the gift, and then we . . ." Chin was clearly envisioning them working as a team.

"I said I don't want your help," repeated Fei Fei.

"But I—" Before Chin could finish, Fei Fei took him by the shoulders and moved him behind her. His shoulders fell. But she wasn't finished.

"I never wanted you on this trip!" snarled Fei Fei. Chin was the only outlet for all of her anxiety and frustration, and she was ready to unload.

"But I . . ." Chin's eyes widened.

"I never even wanted you in my life!" continued Fei Fei. All of her disappointment and anger spilled out of her.

"You can't talk to your brother like that," protested Chin. His chin trembled.

"You're NOT my brother. You will NEVER be my brother," she said with finality. She turned and walked away. Bungee looked at Chin, his face devastated, and then toward Fei Fei's back moving away from them.

For a moment, Chin didn't move. Then slowly, against the tide of the crowd, he headed back to the palace. Bungee followed after him, listening to him talk. "She didn't mean that," Chin told himself. Fei

Fei wanted the photo so much; that's why she was behaving badly. "I just need to get that photo," he decided. It was just a matter of figuring out how. He picked up his step, eager to take on the job.

Fei Fei looked around for her little white rabbit. "Bungee?" she called. Then she brought herself back to the urgent task at hand. She would find Bungee later. "I have to find the gift." She quickened her pace, looking for a vehicle she could use. Of course, there was still the matter of learning how to operate a spaceship.

"Will anybody help me?" Fei Fei asked, half to herself, half to the Lunarians taking off and leaving her behind. Her chance to get the photo was dwindling with the disappearing crowd.

From the orb where she was standing, Fei Fei spotted three tough-looking chickens on motor scooters getting ready to take off. Lunarian biker chickens? Mustering all of her courage, Fei Fei leaped off the orb and landed on the bike of the largest chicken, who was the size of a small car.

His feathers were a brilliant shade of blue. Her sudden appearance made the bike tip over, but the blue chicken quickly set it upright. She heard one of the other chickens call him Bill.

"Can I get a ride?" asked Fei Fei. She used the voice she used when she sold mooncakes. Friendly and confident and not ready to take no for an answer.

"Biker chicks only!" Bill said gruffly. He lifted her off the bike, ready to drop her like an unwanted bug. Fei Fei thought quickly. "Wait! I know where the gift is," she said.

Bill looked at the other two chickens, a chicken whose small head bobbled on top of a long neck that bounced like a spring and an orange chicken who was so round that Fei Fei was tempted to see if it could roll like a ball. They assented, eager to find the gift.

"All right," said Bill.

"Lead the way," said Gretch, the round chicken. Bill put Fei Fei back on the bike in front of him.

The bikes hovered over the ground, glowing green, blue, and pink.

"Okay!" said Fei Fei. They opened the throttles on the bikes and hit the ignition. The engines growled to life. Boots up! The three bikes zoomed across the lunar landscape, leaving a spiral of dust in their wake.

Chapter Seven

Chin and Bungee snuck back into the palace and into the corridor. From behind a column, they watched a group of Moon Guards march through the hall of the main palace in perfect unison. Each Moon Guard, in the shape of a star, carried a staff with a sharp-pointed crescent moon on top. Their faces were stern, unsmiling.

You can be brave, Chin told himself. You can be brave for Fei Fei. He leaned down to Bungee and whispered, "You take that one, and I'll take the rest!" Then he ran into the hallway, screaming fiercely. "Raaaaaaah!"

From out of nowhere, though, a fleet of Shooting Stars zoomed in and began to race around the columns and then swarm around Chin. Their red and blue lights were so bright, they blinded him.

The lights felt hot. The streaks of light had dramatic Chinese opera masks in the front. Unblinking black eyes and snarling open mouths flew by. The closer they came, the scarier they became.

"Ah! Ahhhhh!" screamed Chin. He put up his arms, trying to fight his way out, but the Stars were too quick. They trapped him.

From the top of the long hallway, Chang'e appeared with the Lunettes following behind her. She did not appear to be in any hurry. She observed the boy, his arms pinned down by his sides by the Stars.

"Whoa! What are these things?" cried Chin. One of the Stars zapped Chin for talking. "Ow!" he yelped.

"Palace security," answered Chang'e crisply. Then, as quickly as they had appeared, the Shooting Stars sped into the never-ending ceiling and vanished.

"Whoa," breathed Chin.

"What are you doing here?" asked Chang'e.

He drew himself up and let his loyalty to Fei Fei embolden him. "I want the photo for my sister!" he said firmly.

Chang'e was not moved by this display of brotherly devotion. In fact, she seemed annoyed. "Well, I want the gift," she responded.

"Well, I know where it is!" said Chin, wanting to top her. That was a mistake.

Chang'e flared her nostrils. "Oh you do?" she said. She snapped her fingers. "Bring him to the interrogation chamber."

Interrogation chamber? A door appeared out of nowhere in front of Chin. Chin tried to resist going through the door. "I won't go!" The door to the room opened, and a bright light shot out. "I won't, I won't!" said Chin, twisting his body away from the door. If he went into the room, Chin had a feeling that he would never come out.

But then his eye caught something. Floating down to the middle of the room was . . . a Ping-Pong table!

Chin stopped resisting. "I'm in!" he announced. Croak hopped out of his pocket and into the room. Ping-Pong was, of course, Chin's specialty. He eyed the table eagerly.

"How about a game? You like games?" asked Chang'e. Her voice was soft and dangerous like a tiger's purr.

"You know it!" said Chin, pulling his ever-ready paddle out of his pocket.

The goddess gestured toward the table. "Tell you what—if you win, I'll give you that photo."

Chin's heart leaped. Fei Fei could not be angry at him any longer if he had the photo.

"But if I win, you tell me where the gift is," continued Chang'e.

"Deal," agreed Chin. He was certain he could win. Then again, he had no choice.

Chang'e smiled and lifted her paddle. Her traditional gown transformed into a sky-blue tracksuit with intricate embroidery up and down the sleeves. Her hair went from its elaborate arrangement to

one high ponytail held back by a red headband.

"We'll play by Lunaria rules!" she announced.

With that, the table and the two players began to float in midair. Chin struggled to maintain his balance. His body tipped and wobbled. "Whoa! Whoooa!" he yelped. They took their positions at the opposite ends of the table while around them the room changed into a futuristic arena. The Lunettes cheered for Chang'e as the game commenced. Chang'e and Chin each cried "Qiu! Sha!" when delivering a particularly savage ball across the table for a point. Chin began to think about what strategies to employ; he would need more than just his Ping-Pong skills.

Chang'e quickly garnered three points and began taunting Chin. "Tell me where the gift is," she said. "Or I'll lose my cool."

Chin refused to lose hope. "I'd like to tell," he countered. "But soon that picture will be mine!" Their words flew over the table almost faster than the ball.

"You think you're going to defeat me?" scoffed Chang'e.

"I'm sort of the champion at my table tennis school," said Chin, exaggerating slightly. He puffed out his chest and returned the ball with a flick of his paddle.

"And you have yet to see all the winning talents I have hidden up my sleeve," boasted Chang'e.

Chin held on. "Bring it, sling it, everything you got. I'll battle with my paddle and return your every shot," he chanted.

Chang'e began playing with a dizzying array of moves. "Space serve!" "Moon slams!" "Lava spins!" She announced each new play as the ball played off her paddle, the slightest turn of her wrist changing the spin and direction of the ball. "Give me what I want, or I will seal that door," she threatened. "Tell me where the gift is. I want Houyi here with me."

"You better talk soon, or you'll never leave the dark side of the moon," cooed the Lunettes, their menacing words contrasting with their sweet voices.

Chin decided to fight back—with his own taunts. He thought of the other story of Chang'e he had heard at the New Year's dinner—the one where the goddess had taken the pills out of selfishness.

He returned the ball triumphantly. "But don't you see? If you hadn't been so selfish, Houyi would have immortality." Chang'e's expression changed. He had struck a nerve.

"It's no wonder 'bad haircut' left you," said Chang'e, clearly irritated.

Chin would take no insult of his soon-to-be sister. "She got swept up in the crowd," he explained simply. "And when I get the picture, I will make my sister proud."

At the thought of winning Fei Fei's approval, he redoubled his efforts. He began returning the ball more forcefully, with more cunning. On a scoreboard that had magically appeared, Chin's score began to rise.

"Give me the gift," said Chang'e through gritted teeth. "Or I'll keep you for eternity." She twisted her paddle and aimed the ball directly at Chin's head.

"Ow!" cried Chin as the ball struck him in the forehead.

Chang'e and the Lunettes joined their voices to discourage Chin. "You'll lose. You'll lose." Their words spun around him, so it was hard to tell what was being said and what he was thinking. "Better talk soon, or you'll never leave the dark side of the moon."

The ball seemed to speed up, flying across the table so fast that it was a blur. The game was going into double time. Each player leaned in, refusing to back down.

"I will make this place your destiny," hissed Chang'e, gesturing to the room.

Even Chin would not want to stay in a single room with a Ping-Pong table for the rest of his life. He swallowed his fear and fought back. What had Fei Fei said his superpower was? Being super annoying. He came up with another taunt. "How's it feel to be alone and never see his face?" he asked, referring to Houyi.

"She'll never be your sister," replied Chang'e cruelly. "And when I win, I'll put you in your place." With that, she flipped the table and sent it spinning. Now the game was being played on a whirling table. "Tell me what I need!" she cried as she smashed the ball toward Chin.

He lunged and caught the ball on the edge of his paddle. The force of the ball sent the boy crashing into the wall. He drew in his breath for one last battle cry. "You know what I heard?" Chin shouted. "You're a three-thousand-year-old lady who ate both immortality pills and now you live alone, FOREVER!"

Chin launched the ball off his paddle, sending it high into the air. The ball rose then reversed course, falling toward the table. It struck the corner of the table—it was in. Chang'e swiped at it—and missed.

The scoreboard lit up, "Winner: Chin." The table, now prone to gravity, fell to the floor and cracked into pieces. "I win!" Chin cried triumphantly. He held out his hand, ready to receive the photo as he and the goddess floated back to the ground.

But the goddess did not keep her word. "No one's leaving until I get that gift!" she snarled. She stalked out of the room with the Lunettes following closely behind. The door slammed and locked behind her. Chin ran to the door.

"You can't lock me up! I can run through walls, you know!" shouted Chin. He pounded on the door. But he was trapped.

Chapter Eight

Inside her personal chamber, Chang'e paced back and forth. The Lunettes watched her anxiously. Then the goddess flung herself on the bed and let out a wail. "Uuuuuuggggh!" she cried.

The mooncakes gathered around, trying to soothe her. "Please try to stay calm. You don't want to cause another meteor shower," said Blue Lunette. Whenever Chang'e cried, meteors rained down on the planet, causing all kinds of damage. Everyone feared the meteor showers from Chang'e.

"Do yoga with us!" suggested Yellow Lunette as a distraction.

Pink Lunette inhaled noisily. "Calming breath in . . ."

All three Lunettes took in a long breath at the same time and then assumed a yoga pose. Yellow

Lunette tipped over and rolled off her yoga mat. "Oh boy!" she said.

"Calming breath out . . . ," said Pink Lunette, trying to stay focused. She puckered her lips and blew out.

"I'm calm, I'm calm," said Chang'e, exhaling with the Lunettes. For a moment it worked, but then the Lunettes watched in alarm as clouds and lightning began to form around her head. Chang'e started to sob. As the teardrops fell, they sprouted into little Lunarians, each droplet becoming a different color.

"I'm calm," said Chang'e, though she was clearly not. Then: "Waaaaaah!"

"Oh, oh, goddess!" cried Blue Lunette. It was easier to keep Chang'e happy with compliments and attention; once she started to cry, their job became so much more difficult. The Lunettes and Lunarians fluttered helplessly around their goddess.

At that moment, Jade Rabbit came into the room and shooed out the baby Lunarians. His entrance provided a brief distraction, which was enough to stem the tears.

"Oh . . . hi, Jade," said Chang'e. One last tear fell and formed a Lunarian. The newest Lunarian scuttled away, searching for the others. Exhausted by her own tantrum, Chang'e slumped into an overstuffed chair in the room. The green rabbit hopped into her lap. Chang'e spent a lot of time with the Lunettes, but she was still closer to Jade Rabbit. They had been together the longest.

"Please," pleaded Chang'e "At least tell me that the potion is working." Jade Rabbit frowned and shook his head in frustration. He was good at many things, but he could not figure out the solution to this particular problem.

"I'll never see Houyi again, will I?" asked Chang'e. She didn't wait for an answer. Instead she got up and walked out to the balcony. Sparks flew around her head, gathering energy. She screamed. The air filled with frustration, sadness, anger, and remorse. It was pure pain.

The Lunettes huddled together and transformed themselves back into one large mooncake. In the distance, on the horizon, meteors began to rain down on the moon.

A fireball flash appeared out of nowhere over the Biker Chicks and Fei Fei. "It looks like the Moon Goddess is astronomically upset!" said Lulu. She was the chicken with the long neck.

A cluster of meteors quickly followed, barely missing them. BOOM! BOOM! BOOM! Fei Fei maneuvered the bike past one giant meteor, barely keeping control of the bike. The bike tipped and shuddered, threatening to fall completely on its side. Fei Fei threw her weight to one side and kept the bike upright. A huge explosion thudded behind them, sending shards of rock everywhere. The Biker Chicks steered the bikes through the meteor shower, avoiding the worst of the debris and dirt.

"When she's mad, this road is impossible," said Gretchen.

"Yeah, come on, let's wait it out," said Bill. He might have been the biggest one, but his size didn't make him the most courageous. The chickens looked fearfully at the sky.

"No, we're going," Fei Fei said, taking the lead. "Follow me." She was used to biking with boxes full of mooncakes through bumpy fields, dodging people—she could do this! Fei Fei flicked a switch on the handlebars, and all three bikes leaped into hyperspeed. There was no time for fear. They zoomed into the canyon, a meteor striking the ground where they had been a second before.

"Go left!" commanded Fei Fei as they dodged a meteor following close behind them. "Go right!" she ordered. They turned hard, barely escaping another one. "Okay, now left!" she said. The sound of high-pitched chicken screams echoed through the canyon.

A giant meteor hurtled toward them—this time directly at Fei Fei and Bill. "We've gotta get through that canyon!" Fei Fei said, pointing to a canyon behind the approaching meteor. She leaned forward, trying to coax every bit of speed out of the bike.

"WHOA! We're not going to make it! We're not going to make it!" Bill screeched.

"Don't be such a chicken!" Fei Fei said. She punched the accelerator at the last second and launched the bike over the meteor. The heat from the explosion scorched the bottoms of her feet.

"Aaaaaah!" screamed Bill.

"Woohoohoo!" screamed Fei Fei. They were having the same experience but different reactions. We're still alive, she thought, and getting closer to the rocket. They just needed to outlast the meteor storm.

"Yaaaaa!" cheered Gretchen. She let out a whistle. The air was growing calm again. The meteors were tapering off. They had survived.

"Let's get that gift!" said Fei Fei. The Biker Chicks revved their engines and drove off, leaving the craters made by the meteors in the dust.

The crash site came into view. "There it is!" Fei Fei shouted. "Over there! My rocket ship!"

The spaceship lay in pieces across the lunar landscape. Fei Fei took in a sharp breath. It was hard to believe that after all her hard work, the rocket had shattered into pieces. "Ugh . . . oh . . . my rocket ship," she mourned. She got off her bike and approached the site on foot. She looked sadly at the bits and pieces of the rocket ship, but she did not have time to think too much about it. She did not have time to do anything but look for the gift, whatever it was.

"What a mess," Bill said.

"What's this gift look like anyway?" Gretch said.

"I'm not sure," Fei Fei said. "Let's spread out. We'll find it."

She scanned the ground and noticed a rectangle drifting along. She knelt down and flipped it over. It was the picture of her, Baba, and Mama that she had taped to the dashboard! Seeing the photo renewed her—it was almost as though she could

feel Mama's embrace, hear their laughter together, just by looking at the photo. She was going to find the gift, whatever and wherever it was.

Fei Fei moved closer to the crashed spaceship and saw something sitting on a cart, wrapped in a cape and with a space helmet on. The cart moved toward her, propelled by an unseen force. The creature stood up and fell clumsily into her arms. His small body glowed green from his long snout to his tail. He stood on two legs, which brought him to Fei Fei's waist.

"Kooophaaa, pehhh, kaahhhh," said the creature. He was making weird breathing noises. "Ah! Whoa! Whoa! Whoa!"

His visor quickly flipped up to reveal a green glowy roly-poly creature with a superlong tongue. "Hi, I'm Gobi. What's your name?" he said. His voice was cheerful and rubbery. It reminded Fei Fei of gummi bears.

"I'm . . . Fei Fei," she said.

"Hi, I'm Gobi. What's your name?" he repeated.

Fei Fei blinked. She didn't know how to respond to that.

But Gobi did. "I feel like we are talking in a circle," he said quickly. "I actually used to be a nervous talker, and I think that's what's really great about me is that, like, I'm so self-aware of my nervous talking. Though I got to slow it down, relax, and just breathe. I'm checking my pulse right now . . . ah! Serenity achieved."

"Who are you?" Fei Fei asked. "*What* are you?"

Gobi seemed a tad insulted by this. He squared his shoulders. "I happen to be Chang'e's most trusted adviser. Very high-level, uh, member of the court! I mean, not a like a court jester, but definitely a member of the court, like, really high up. I'm basically indispensable."

"Then what are you doing all the way out here?" Fei Fei asked. Before Gobi could answer he was yanked back as the lunar rover trudged over his cape.

"Wait!" Fei Fei said, "Is that *the* lunar rover with my parachute?"

"I dunno," Gobi said as the rover began to roll away with the parachute. "Hey!" Gobi said. "You can take my cape, but I'm keeping these sweet moon pants!"

Fei Fei could not quite bring herself to continue to talk to this strange being, even though she had met many odd creatures. She didn't even have the heart to tell him that those moon pants were diapers. She had to stay on task. She turned to continue looking through the remains of the rocket ship, but Gobi followed her.

"What are you doing out here?" he asked. Gobi had a very long tongue that bounced out of his mouth as if it had a mind of its own. The tongue wiggled around.

"It's a long story," said Fei Fei, not wanting to get distracted from her task.

"A story!" Gobi gasped. His eyes widened, as if he could not imagine a more delightful answer. "A story! Are you kid— Oh my go— A story!" He took a deep breath. "Ohhhh nooooo, no one has told me a story in a thousand years. That would be amazing." He struck a reclining pose on the ground. "Ready!"

"Hey, what's he doing here?" demanded one of the chickens. The chickens did not seem pleased to see Gobi. "I wouldn't be talking to that one if I were you."

"Yeah, he was exiled from the palace by the goddess!" said Lulu. She knocked Gobi's helmet off with a hard strike. Although Fei Fei was not sure how she felt about Gobi, she did not like Lulu being so mean to him.

"Exiled from the palace?" Fei Fei asked Gobi.

"He-he, don't listen to these Lunarian chickens. They're a bit scrambled up," said Gobi nervously. He lowered his voice. "They are bad eggs."

"Look who's talking!" The chickens' voices blended and merged.

"Yeah! You little green glowworm!" said Bill. He gave Gobi a hard peck. The chickens began to laugh meanly.

Fei Fei tried to regain control of the situation.

"Quit wasting time," she said. "We need to find the gift for Chang'e."

"Chang'e?" Gobi's voice rose in excitement. "I wanna help! I'd love to help! Did I mention I could help?" His body began to change colors quickly.

"Maybe this could be the gift!" Gretch tore a window off the rocket as she spoke. The chickens began destroying the rest of the rocket ship.

Fei Fei spotted something sticking up out of the dust behind a piece of wreckage. Could it be? She picked it up, first cautiously, then clutched the object in excitement. Her Chang'e doll!

"What'd you find there?" asked Gretch.

"Oh! My doll!" said Fei Fei. She couldn't believe she had found the doll her mother had given her; she had assumed the doll had been lost in the crash. She straightened the doll's robes fondly and brushed off the dirt. She thought of Mama's stories of Chang'e, of Space Dog, as Fei Fei held the doll by the canal. "I can't believe I almost lost this." Then an idea clicked for Fei Fei. It would make sense, for a gift for Chang'e to be a doll that looked like her. "Something my mama gave me as a *gift*."

She had scarcely finished saying the last word when Gretch leaned over and snatched the doll away from Fei Fei. In one quick motion, Gretch jumped on her bike.

"Are we leaving already?" asked Fei Fei, confused.

Gretch gave Fei Fei a crafty look. "Whoever gets to the goddess *first* with the gift gets their wish granted." Fei Fei looked at the chickens, mouth open. She could not believe they were betraying her, after all they had been through together.

The other two chickens opened the throttles on their bikes. Bill shot Fei Fei a quick look. "Sorry," he muttered.

"Hammer down!" ordered Lulu.

"No! That's mine! COME BACK!" pleaded Fei Fei. But she was powerless to stop them. She tried to run after them, but they were too fast. "Don't do this to me," she begged. She was so close, she could not fail now.

She watched the bikers grow smaller and smaller until they became a dot that disappeared. Gobi turned and looked at Fei Fei hopefully. She began walking. Gobi trailed after her.

"Sorry, I've gotta find some mean chickens and get back to Lunaria," she said, hoping Gobi would take the hint and let her walk alone.

"Lunaria?" repeated Gobi. The two jumped down the side of a crater. "Well, you'll need a guide. And guess what? This guy used to both work and live at the palace." Gobi pointed to himself with what Fei Fei assumed were his thumbs.

"You worked in the palace?" she asked, raising one eyebrow.

"Yeah huh," said Gobi, nodding. He kept pace with her, showing no signs of backing off.

Fei Fei set her jaw. "As soon as I get my gift back, I'm taking it to Chang'e," she said.

Gobi threw himself in front of her. "A gift? Oh, please let me help you bring a gift to the goddess!"

"No," said Fei Fei.

"Please????" begged Gobi.

"No," said Fei Fei more firmly.

"Please???????"

"No!"

"Pleeeeeee———"

"No!" shouted Fei Fei.

"Let me finish," said Gobi. "—eeeeeeeeeeeeeeee eeeeeeeeeeeeeeeeeeeee——!"

The sound was so terrible that Fei Fei had to cover her ears. It was a ghastly sound, screechy and loud, and seemingly unending.

"Okay, okay!" she shouted over the squealing. "Just stop making that noise!"

Gobi talked as he and Fei Fei made their way across the moon. Some people enjoy silences. Gobi was not one of them. His voice rattled and bumped along steadily.

"I actually used to be a nervous talker, but I'm starting to work on that. I realized, 'Wow, I am talking really fast,' and I thought to myself, You should relax. So I've been working on slowing it down and breathing and— Uh-oh— AH!"

Gobi's long tongue had tied itself up through all of his talking. "Sometimes it causes me to get a little tongue-tied," he said—or tried to say, with the knots in his tongue. It sounded like "a libbuh tum-tibeb." The rest of Gobi got tangled up in his tongue. He lost his balance and fell backward into a crater.

Fei Fei shook her head and carefully helped him back on his feet. Then she untangled his tongue. He slurped his tongue back into his mouth. "Urgh! I hate when this happens!" he said.

Suddenly, the ground began to rumble. It shook so hard that it jolted their feet. Gobi let out a high-pitched scream. They were going higher and higher into the air. They tumbled off the mound of Earth.

It was an army of moon frogs. Enormous, slimy moon frogs, and they had been nesting inside the crater that Gobi had fallen into. They let out a chorus of croaks as they began to move.

"Gobi, what's happening?" asked Fei Fei. The

frogs seemed to be searching for something. Maybe food?

"They just woke up from hibernation. Happens this time every year!" noted Gobi. His comments did not assure Fei Fei. Maybe the giant amphibians would eat *them* after a long hibernation. Did frogs have teeth, or would they be swallowed whole?

One frog appeared to be the leader. It turned, wiggled its rear, and leaped over another giant frog. In one bound, the frog had gone as high as a house and as far as a soccer field. The other frogs turned and followed.

The frogs' enormous legs could smash a car flat, and they probably won't even notice. Their gaping mouths were just as large. Fei Fei wouldn't be their dinner; she'd be just a light snack. She watched the frogs leap over one another, trying to not make a sound.

"They're on their way to Lunaria Lake to feed," Gobi told Fei Fei. She relaxed. The frogs had better food to eat.

As Fei Fei watched the frogs jump an idea began to form in her mind. "Hey, I know this game," she said. Then she turned and said to Gobi, "Sorry about this. . . ."

She grabbed Gobi's long tongue, swung it over her head, and like a lasso, looped Gobi's tongue over one of the moon frogs passing by.

"Hold on!" shouted Fei Fei. She held tightly on to Gobi and pulled the two of them onto the back of the frog. The frog was moving in a long, easy rhythm, tensing and springing, tensing and springing. It didn't seem like they were moving that fast, but of course, the frog was so large that they were.

"Not a bad way to travel," remarked Fei Fei as they adjusted to the frog's movement.

Gobi retracted his tongue back into his mouth. They watched the landscape around them from their new perch, relaxing temporarily.

"Ah, good times," said Gobi. "Good times." He let out a breath and settled into the cushion of the frog's back.

Fei Fei looked over at the creature and felt a stab of compassion. Gobi clearly had been alone for a long time and was a bit desperate for company. "So, why were you living by yourself?" she asked.

"That's a personal question," said Gobi. Then, unable to *not* talk, he relented. "But, since you and I are like family now, I can tell you. It happened a long time ago. The goddess exiled me from Lunaria because of a song I sang to her."

Fei Fei was horrified. Even for a goddess as fickle as Chang'e, that seemed extreme. "She exiled you over a song? That's terrible."

"Not compared to what happened next," said Gobi. He leaned forward. "The goddess disappeared. All the lights in Lunaria went out. We call it the big darkness. It was awful." He hung his head at the memory, ashamed that he had caused it.

Fei Fei tried to comfort him. "Chang'e isn't anything like what I thought she'd be," she offered, thinking of when she was little and Chang'e seemed so beautiful.

"Well, I do," Gobi sang. "It changes every day. It spins and turns and twirls away. It just keeps rollin' on and that is wonderful!" With each word, the song became lovelier and more powerful. Now Fei Fei was catching on to the meaning of Gobi's song. It was about change, changes in colors, changes in the sky, changes in time. Things changed, whether she wanted them to or not.

"I just want things to go back to how they were," said Fei Fei softly.

The frogs lit up in a gorgeous display. Fei Fei curled up on the frog's back, unwilling to take in any more of the song. Gobi sang the last part of the song directly to Fei Fei.

Do you ever feel afraid?
Curl up when you are hurting?
And hold your memories tight to you?
Yeah, me too.
If you release the past
You'll move ahead and bloom at last.

The heart grows
And it knows
You can glow. You're wonderful.

The song ended on a graceful note. Fei Fei felt at peace, a feeling she had not had in a long time. "So . . . that's the song you sang to her?"

"No, it was another song," deadpanned Gobi.

"Gobi . . . ," said Fei Fei.

"Yeah," admitted Gobi. "That's the song." He looked pleased with himself, and a little sad. They both laughed.

The moon frogs were listening, too. Feeling renewed, they all approached the glowing city of Lunaria in the distance.

Chapter Nine

In Lunaria, Bungee was watching Jade Rabbit from her hiding place in the palace.

Jade Rabbit hopped down one hallway, carrying a small object in his paws, followed by a formation of uniformed marching mooncakes. Bungee headed down the same hallway, careful to avoid detection. As the guards continued on their way, she watched Jade Rabbit thump out a pattern on the floor. Then, to her surprise, a secret passage in the floor opened up. Jade Rabbit disappeared into the opening, and quickly, quietly, Bungee slipped in behind the green rabbit.

The passage led to the rabbitory, an underground lab. The rabbitory was filled with glowing plants, colorful test tubes, and bubbling beakers. Bungee watched as Jade Rabbit gathered ingredients and used a mortar and pestle to grind a sparking powder. It was all an impressive display of scientific prowess—until the powder exploded in his face. His long legs were knocked out from under him as he landed on his small furry behind.

Bungee let out a giggle. Her laughter startled Jade Rabbit—so much so that he bumped into the mortar. The mortar tipped over, threatening to spill the contents. Bungee scurried over and put the bowl back upright.

She looked up at Jade Rabbit. Jade Rabbit perked up his ears and stared back at her. It was as though an electrical current was running between the two, connecting them and filling them with sparks.

Jade Rabbit turned back to his work, trying his best to ignore Bungee and stay on task. There was not much more time to complete the job for Chang'e, and all of his attempts so far had been failures. But it was hard to pretend Bungee wasn't there, especially when she was watching so attentively. He held out the pestle for her to hold while he got another mixture.

With a flick of his paw, he tossed the new mixture into the air and *poof*! Tiny butterflies appeared in the air, hovering and fluttering. They landed on Bungee's nose and then turned back into dust. Bungee accidentally inhaled the dust and then, *achoo!* She let out an adorable sneeze. The sneeze was followed by lasers shooting out of her ears!

Lasers! Bungee clapped her paws together; now she had a personal form of protection. She hopped over to Jade Rabbit and offered a thank-you in the form of rubbing his nose with her nose.

Jade Rabbit's cheeks reddened, but a huge smile spread under his whiskers. With this newfound inspiration, Jade Rabbit got back to work. He returned to the powder in the mortar and concentrated. But something in the air had changed. Maybe it was Bungee's attention and appreciation creating a different kind of magic. This time, when Jade Rabbit added the final ingredient, the potion finally began to glow.

It worked! The potion was ready!

• • •

In a different part of the palace, Chang'e held the lunar hologram in her palm, showing how little time was left. The moon was just the tiniest sliver now. The Lunarians brought in her robe, and the Lunettes draped it over her shoulders.

Chang'e paced in front of a portrait of herself with Houyi. She spoke to the picture. "Houyi, remember when we got married?" She slid her arms into the sleeves. "We promised to share our wings and weave our life together." She sighed. She had just a few minutes to make things right but an eternity for regret.

She raised her chin and began to sing. She sang the words of their wedding vows, her voice aching with the promise of the words.

I am yours forever
Till the end of time
Always and forever
In this heart of mine

Longer than the heavens
And the stars that shine
I am yours
I am yours
Forever

Jade Rabbit entered on quiet feet. Chang'e welcomed the distraction. "Jade?" asked Chang'e.
"What's going on with you? Your fur is extra soft
today and surprisingly swirly."

The green rabbit ducked his head and then
looked bashfully at the goddess. Then, beaming
with pride, he held up a bottle of the glowing
potion. Chang'e gasped. She knelt down so she
was at his height and carefully took the potion
from him with both hands. The glowing liquid
reflected in her large dark eyes. Jade Rabbit could
not tell her that being with Bungee, that love had
been the missing ingredient, but it showed in
everything about him, from his extrasoft fur to
the excited sparkle in his eyes.

"Jade! You—you've done it! And just in time! Now all we need is the gift," she said. The two turned and looked at the portrait together—would all the pieces come together in time?

From the back of their moon frog, Fei Fei and Gobi spotted the bikers in the distance. The bikers were near the lake outside of Lunaria. As the moon frogs closed the distance, Fei Fei could spot her doll on the back of Gretch's bike.

"Don't worry," said Gobi. "I got this!" He shot his tongue out, aiming for the doll. Instead, though, he latched on to Gretch herself, causing her to lose her balance. She zoomed forward, yanking Fei Fei and Gobi off the moon frog and sending them skimming along the lake below. Gobi's stomach began to swell as he filled up with lake water.

Gretch accelerated harder, determined to get to Chang'e first. The Biker Chickens sped upward toward Lunaria. The change in speed knocked the doll off the bike, and it landed on Fei Fei's face. Fei Fei tried to grab for the doll, but she could not get a grip on it. Everyone—Gretch, Gobi, Fei Fei, and the doll—were free-falling while Gobi spewed out water like a faucet. The doll went from hand to claw to hand as they fought and clutched for the doll.

Fei Fei and Gobi landed in Lunaria on one of the buildings with a bouncy roof, but Gretch missed the roof. Instead, she pulled Fei Fei and Gobi off the building as she fell past them. Gobi landed on a Lunarian with a loud splat, much to the horror of a group of bystanders. The squashed Lunarian split and then turned into many little Lunarians. The newly formed creatures cheered. "Awww, hey, little guys," said Gobi, taking a moment to welcome them.

Meanwhile, Fei Fei had landed, unseen, on a roof of a different building. She could hear the chickens nearby searching for the doll.

"Where is it?" asked Gretch.

"It fell somewhere around here."

"Keep looking!" ordered Gretch.

Fei Fei leaped from rooftop to rooftop, conducting her own search and rescue operation. Running on Lunarian roofs was not like running on any surface she was accustomed to. The roof pulled under her feet, so she stayed in place like on a treadmill. The building began to tilt, just as Fei Fei spotted the doll. *Right there.*

It was just out of reach. And then it fell. Fei Fei slid down the side of one building, grabbing on to the tendrils that grew up from the bottom of the building. She reached out and grabbed the doll! It was hers!

And then it wasn't. The doll was jerked roughly out of her hands. Gretch had snatched the doll away.

"Mine!" she announced.

"Hey!" cried Fei Fei.

The chicken laughed. Fei Fei lost her grip on the tendril and started to fall. Gobi looked on in horror. Fei Fei fell into a passing Lunarian spaceship.

The spaceship raced over Gretch's head. The wind was roaring in Fei Fei's ears from going so fast, but she was not going to give up. She loomed near the chicken and made a grab for the doll with one hand.

It turned into a tug-of-war battle, with Fei Fei and Gretch yanking the doll back and forth as they raced down the busy highway, Fei Fei in the space-ship and Gretch on her bike.

"Give me my doll!" cried Fei Fei.

"It's mine!" insisted Gretch.

"Give it back!" said Fei Fei.

"Get your grubby mitts off it!"

Massive deadly energy lines loomed up. The white lines were capable of slicing anything that came near them, and Gretch and Fei Fei were heading straight for them. But neither of them would give up. "Fei Fei! Let go!" screamed Gobi.

At the last second, Gretch bailed on the tug-of-war battle. She leaped off her bike right before the lines. Fei Fei held on to the doll as the spaceship zipped directly into the deadly lines. There was no way to avoid the collision.

A sickening silence followed. The Biker Chickens looked down in shame and then zoomed off, unwilling to get more involved. Gobi, ever the loyal friend, forced himself to go look. He ran toward the lines, hoping against hope. "Fei Fei?" he called.

"Come out, Fei Fei! I'll do anything to make you okay, anything!" he promised. "What do I have to do?" His pleas for the impossible were met with a heartbreaking silence.

And then—a voice.

"Look up!"

Gobi looked upward. There, hanging under a broken piece of building, was Fei Fei, holding herself flat with her hands and feet. She was very much alive. She climbed down to a happily waiting Gobi.

Their joy was short lived, though. Fei Fei had

survived, but the doll had not. Fei Fei scanned the ground. Pieces of the doll were scattered everywhere, too many to count. Her gift to Chang'e was gone.

Chapter Ten

Fei Fei and Gobi sat on a bridge overlooking Lunaria Lake. Fei Fei's head was in her hands. She was grateful to be alive but still frustrated. She was no closer to her goal than she was when she had landed on the moon.

"Why, why, did I ever let those bikers into my life? I've lost everything now." Fei Fei moaned. As her head sank lower and lower, her words became sadder and sadder.

Gobi rummaged through Fei Fei's backpack, looking for something that might cheer her up. "Not everything. You still have this . . . and this . . . and . . ." He accidentally dropped one of the precious things into the water. Oops. He thought quickly. "And you're not dead! That's a plus."

He used his long nose to rummage through her

backpack, hoping to find something else to cheer the girl. He carefully set on the bench her phone, a lamp, map, and mooncake tin—all things she had dumped from her desk drawer into the backpack. Fei Fei did not bother to look.

"That doll was my only chance to get back home and stop my father from getting remarried," she said. She threw a rock into the lake, where it landed with a plop. There was no way that demanding Chang'e would accept as a gift a mended doll or a doll in pieces.

Gobi's mouth dropped open. "Remarried? You mean your mother is . . . I mean, is she . . . um . . . ?" He struggled to find the right and difficult words.

Fei Fei nodded. "She was my sun, my moon, and my stars. And the only person who ever really listened to me." She looked off into the distance, as if trying to find her mother in the sky.

"I'll listen to you," offered Gobi gently.

Fei Fei laid out her situation. "The gift is in pieces. And now I'm not going to get my wish to

stop my dad from marrying that awful woman with her horrible boy."

"What horrible boy?" Gobi looked around as if he had missed the boy in question.

"A ridiculously annoying boy," she said, amending her first description. None of this would have happened if it weren't for Mrs. Zhong and Chin!

"Nobody likes annoying creatures! They are the worst," said Gobi. In his eagerness to be sympathetic, Gobi conveniently forgot that sometimes many people considered Gobi to be annoying.

"He's always making faces," complained Fei Fei, ticking off Chin's many faults. "He plays leapfrog all the time. He thinks he can hang upside down, like a bat, and run through walls. And he's always interrupt—"

"He plays leapfrog?" asked Gobi, interrupting. "Is that where you got the idea for us to ride on those frogs?"

"No!" said Fei Fei, shocked at the suggestion. But where had she gotten the idea? "I mean, not really."

"And he hangs upside down like a bat, like you did from the bridge? Is that where you got that idea?" asked Gobi eagerly.

"No! Urgh. Anyway, I can't stand him," concluded Fei Fei.

"I can't stand him either," said Gobi, ever loyal to her. Then, still curious, he added, "Did you say he can run through walls?"

"Forget it, all right?" snapped Fei Fei.

"I would love to have a brother. But then, I've been alone for a thousand years. How many years have you been alone?" asked Gobi.

"Four." Was four years a long time or a short time? Fei Fei could not decide.

"Well, give it time. You might change your mind," he suggested. He looked up at Fei Fei with his large brown eyes.

"Never," said Fei Fei. She sank down into her own body. Everything seemed hopeless.

"I think Miss Grumpy-Pants is hungry," said Gobi, trying to change the subject. "Why don't we eat something?" He went back to the backpack. "Everything looks better when your tummy is full. Oooh! There's a tasty map right here!" He held up the paper map and helped himself to a bite. The paper made a loud tearing sound. "Mmm, delicious. Have some map!"

Fei Fei bypassed the reportedly delicious map and instead picked up the tin with the mooncake. She opened it and took a small bite.

"Yech, I can't believe you eat mooncakes," said Gobi, still munching on the map. He made a face. "That's barbaric."

"Our mooncakes don't have feelings," Fei Fei reminded him. She took another bite and then stopped. "Ow! What's this?"

She had bitten something hard inside the mooncake. Fei Fei pulled out a small broken piece of metal. The shard was covered with strange engravings.

"It's a lunar tick. They're crazy good!" Gobi grabbed the piece of metal and popped it into his mouth. Then he spat it out. "Definitely not."

Fei Fei grabbed the piece back. "Looks like the broken half of something. Chin probably found it somewhere and thought it would be funny to bake it into a mooncake. I told you he's annoying." In her mind, not only were the things Chin did annoying, but anything that was annoying was probably done by Chin!

Gobi inspected the metal bit more closely. "Wait a minute—why does this look familiar?" he asked. He held it up to take a closer look. When he held it in the air, the strange engravings lined up perfectly with a symbol on a building across the street. The symbols were all over Lunaria. "Nope, never seen it," announced Gobi cluelessly.

Fei Fei took the shard back and held it up against the symbol across the street. From her view, she could see that the half piece of metal formed a whole with the symbol.

Gobi could see it now, too. Their jaws dropped open. They stared at the metal piece and then stared at each other. Fei Fei heard her mother's words. *Magic in these mooncakes for you.* Was this part of the magic? Could it be? Gobi started glowing from the inside, a rainbow of colors flashing around. Then they could not contain their excitement any longer.

"This amulet, Gobi! It's the gift!" squealed Fei Fei. He laughed. Their problem was solved—or was it? They looked out over Lunaria toward the clock above the palace. Only the tiniest thread of time was left.

"There's still a chance," said Fei Fei. "We've gotta get this to Chang'e! Come on!" She grabbed Gobi, and together they raced toward the palace.

Back inside the palace, Chin was pondering his own problem. He was still trapped in the room that Chang'e had left him in. He bounced a ball on his Ping-Pong paddle, thinking. "I gotta get outta here! We gotta help Fei Fei!" He had already tried multiple times to get out and had plenty of bumps and bruises to mark his failures. But he could not stop trying. He would not stop trying, for Fei Fei.

He took a few steps back from the closest wall and assumed a runner's start, his body tense and low to the ground. He squinted at the wall and leaned forward a bit more. Then he let out a cry as he sprang toward the wall.

"NO BARRIERS!!!! RAHHHH!" He ran straight at the wall.

After so many failed attempts, Chin was shocked to find himself passing through the wall without a scratch! Suddenly, he was in the hallway among bits of broken wall.

"I did it!" he exclaimed. He looked around, and from the wreckage, a small white figure emerged. Her ear tips were glowing, with trails of smoke coming out of the ends.

"Bungee!" Chin could scarcely do more than gape at the rabbit. He took a closer look at her ears. She blew out the smoke like a cowboy with a six-shooter. It seemed that Bungee had gained some new powers while Chin was locked up. "Maybe *we* did it," he admitted. Perhaps he had needed Bungee's help to get out.

There wasn't any more time to admire their handiwork, though. They were on a mission.

Bungee and Chin moved near the Hallway of Shooting Stars, which was streaked with burning comet trails. Chin remembered the last time they had encountered the hostile beings—they were the ones who had trapped him. He pulled out his Ping-Pong paddle, and Bungee recharged her ears. Sparks began to fly out. This time, he and Bungee would be more prepared.

"Let's do this!" he hollered. "Raaaaah!" As soon as they entered the hallway, the Shooting Stars began their attack, diving and zooming near Chin and Bungee. But this time, the boy and the rabbit were ready to fight back. Bungee used her laser ears to zap the Shooting Stars. Pow! Zap! Ping! Her lasers detonated the stars on contact in midair so that they could not hurt anyone. Chin took on the remaining Shooting Stars, batting them away with his Ping-Pong paddle.

"Rah! Zap! Gotcha! Haha!" said Chin jubilantly. He swung and parried with the Stars. Then, Chin and Bungee darted away, heading deeper into the palace. They ran around a corner, where they found . . .

Fei Fei!

Fei Fei had made it to the palace! There was a strange creature with her, looking shyly at him, but first Chin focused all his attention on Fei Fei. The words tumbled out of Chin. "Fei Fei! Oh my gosh, I'm so happy to see you!" he cried. He was so happy that Fei Fei almost forgot to be annoyed with him.

"Chin," she said, her voice thick with emotion. "I have the gift!" Then she spotted Bungee. "Bungee!" The rabbit hopped into her arms, her ears sparking. Fei Fei gave her a warm hug. They had to keep moving, though. Time was slipping by. Chin tried to give Fei Fei an update as they ran to the throne room. He described the Ping-Pong game against Chang'e and how he ended up trapped in the room.

"It was so crazy! The poles were all moving, and then I was surrounded! I was trying to get the photo for you because I really want to be your brother. And then I saw . . ." He stopped as he moved closer to the creature that had come with Fei Fei. They had not been introduced.

"Hi, I'm Gobi. I just returned from a thousand years in exile," he said, for once opting to go with the short version. "I wonder if I'll run into anyone I kn—" He was suddenly tackled by the palace guards in the shape of mooncakes. They had not forgotten about Gobi, even after a thousand years.

"The amulet!" Fei Fei shouted. Gobi tossed it to her. Fei Fei dropped the amulet, and it slipped across the ground.

"Go on without me," he urged.

Fei Fei scrambled to get the amulet, but they were not going to leave Gobi behind either. Fei Fei and Chin ran back and pried Gobi away from the guards. The Lunettes appeared just as they escaped.

"Oh, hurry, come this way!" said Yellow Lunette urgently.

"Come on, she's waiting for you," said Blue Lunette. There was no question who "she" was in the sentence. The Lunettes guided Fei Fei, Chin, Bungee, and Gobi to the throne room.

"Goddess!" one of them cried. "It's here!"

Chapter Eleven

"Goddess! It's here!" announced the Lunettes.

Fei Fei ran up the long, curving staircase to meet Chang'e. The goddess was surrounded by a crowd of Lunarians who were eager to see what would happen next. Chang'e turned and made her way down the stairs to meet her. She looked at Fei Fei expectantly.

Fei Fei bowed and held up the amulet with both hands. "I think this is the gift you are looking for," she said. Her words did not reflect all the struggle and heartache she had endured for this moment, and yet they were enough.

Chang'e smiled, pure joy radiating from her face. She carefully examined the amulet in her delicate hands. "Of course," she said with amazement. "The other half of my necklace." It made sense that this would be the gift, one object that completed another. The Lunarians cheered. Their queen would finally be allowed the happiness she had been denied for so long.

"What about the photograph?" asked Chin. He had not forgotten why Fei Fei had come to see Chang'e in the first place. But Fei Fei shushed him. For Chang'e, time was quickly running out; Fei Fei could get the photo later.

Chang'e picked up her robes and began making her way back up the stairs. Chang'e continued her way to the center of the hall, where Jade Rabbit was waiting.

"Our two halves are whole again," announced Chang'e. "You can come back to me." She connected the two halves, and placed the now-whole amulet on the center of an ornate pedestal. Then Jade Rabbit stepped forward to work his magic.

The entire room held its breath to see if the amulet would work. Faint music, mysterious and beautiful, filled the hall. Slowly but surely, the amulet began to float up in the air. But that was not the only transformation.

Fei Fei looked on in amazement as the banquet hall began to change. Lush, green grass sprouted up from the floor, accompanied by flowers of every shape and color imaginable. The pillars in the hall turned into trees, and Fei Fei could hear birds rustling in the leaves. The throne room had become a magical forest.

The goddess herself began to rise into the air. Light filled, wispy clouds washed over her, turning her back into her likeness on Earth. Chang'e began the incantation, their wedding vows, calling to Houyi, promising to always love him, through time, through space. Her enchanting voice held both sorrow and promise.

I am yours forever
Till the end of time
Always and forever
In this heart of mine

Longer than the heavens
And the stars that shine
I am yours
I am yours forever

And then incredibly, a male voice joined the last line. Their voices blended and lifted, her sweeter pitch combining with his deeper tones.

Then, a figure began to float down from the dark recesses of the palace ceiling. Was it really possible? As the figure began to take on a more definite form, Chang'e dared to say her heart's fondest wish.

"Houyi?" she asked.

The figure transformed from faint to definite but transparent. Light flowed out. It was Houyi. He was a handsome man, with broad shoulders and thoughtful, deep-set eyes. "But we will be together," he promised, taking over the song.

Chang'e looked into the eyes of her beloved. His eyes revealed a man who had suffered terrible loss but still chose love, still loved Chang'e. They sang the last part of the song together, promising to always love each other, to belong to one another. Fei Fei and the rest of the room watched in wonder, honored to be witnesses to such love.

Chang'e and Houyi fell into an embrace. They did not see the crowd around them, only each other. To see them was to see love itself, in all its strength, weakness, tenderness, and beauty.

"At last," murmured Chang'e. "After all these years."

"Chang'e," said Houyi. He repeated the last sentence of their vows. "I am yours forever," he told her. His voice was gentle but pained. "Chang'e, I cannot stay, but our love is forever."

Then, just as he had appeared, Houyi began to fade away. His hands melted away from Chang'e's hands.

"No! My love!" cried Chang'e. She grasped at the air, trying to stop him. "Please don't leave me again! Don't go! HOUYI!" Her shrieks filled the palace, but her words did nothing to stop his departure. He had not come to return, but rather he had come for the chance to say goodbye. In a few more breaths, Houyi was gone.

Chang'e bowed her head, unable to hold herself up. She looked smaller and more fragile than she ever had. The air in the room changed. This time it was heavy, almost suffocating. A wind began to blow through the hall. The light dimmed. In a few moments, the sound of wind, howling and demanding, began to fill the hall, pulling at the flowers and grasses and trees and threatening to destroy everything in its path. Houyi's departure had created an emptiness that nature itself would try to fill.

Outside, in Lunaria, the city lights went out. Then, within seconds, the entire city plunged into darkness.

"It's the darkness!" cried Gobi, remembering the last, terrible time this happened. The soft inner light that usually filled Gobi and the Lunarians began to fade. Without the light, they were becoming weak.

"Oh no!" said Gobi, right before his light extinguished.

"What's happening?" asked Chin.

Fei Fei tried to explain. "Houyi never became immortal, like Chang'e. Even though their love will last forever, they cannot be together." She did not need to say the last part, that the disappearance of light was Chang'e losing her last bit of hope.

Jade Rabbit sat alone on the stage. Bungee hopped up to him, trying to provide comfort. Fei Fei and Chin joined them.

"Where is she?" asked Fei Fei. At some point in the darkness, the goddess had disappeared completely.

One of the Lunettes answered. "The Chamber of Exquisite Sadness. It's impenetrable. Only the goddess can go in there." Even the Lunettes could not muster their usual encouraging attitude at this time.

Fei Fei raised her chin. She knew what it was like to be alone with sadness. The feeling of emptiness in the room had not frightened her as much as it felt familiar. "Let me try," she said.

The Lunettes walked the group to the Chamber of Exquisite Sadness. Fei Fei had been expecting a room, but it was the opposite of a room with defined walls, floor, and ceiling. It was as if infinity began at the end of the hallway, with the darkness of space spreading in all directions. Millions of tiny points of light hung like crystals on a chandelier in the darkness.

In the midst of this, the tiny figure of Chang'e floated. It felt as if she could slip away at any moment, into the vastness of space, because she had no anchor to hold her. The group stopped, awestruck. "Oh, there she is," said Blue Lunette.

Chin banged on the barrier that separated them from the chamber. His violent efforts made no difference. But when Fei Fei held up her hand to touch the barrier, ever so gently, her arm passed through the wall. The rest of the group watched in alarm as Fei Fei's arm moved between their world and the vast darkness.

"What?" exclaimed Gobi. "That's impossible."

"No! If you go in there, you may never come out again," warned Blue Lunette.

Gobi remembered Fei Fei's strongest motivation. "You may never go home again," he reminded her. With that, she pulled her arm back. She looked at Chin, Gobi, and everyone else around her, one by one. But then she looked back at Chang'e floating alone inside the chamber.

It was not force that allowed her to go through the wall; it was understanding. It was what comes from knowing that the other person knows how you feel.

"No!" said Blue Lunette.

"Wait, Fei Fei!" pleaded Chin. They were all afraid of the chamber, of getting lost, or worse, losing someone precious.

This time, Fei Fei did not hesitate. She put her hand back through the wall, into the chamber, and then entered completely into the infiniteness of the chamber. She could touch the tiny points of light. She moved toward Chang'e.

"Chang'e?" she said. "It's me, Fei Fei, Unfortunate Hair Girl. I'm here to bring you back." At the sound of her voice, Chang'e opened her eyes.

Fei Fei meant to move to Chang'e, but with each step she took toward the goddess, she felt a terrible despair clutch at her soul. Every thought of hope or happiness had disappeared, replaced by nothingness. The chamber seemed to sing a mournful tune, and the air became colder. Fei Fei struggled to keep moving, not because of any outer force holding her back, but because part of her inside was giving up.

Then the lights around her rearranged themselves into constellations. A shape began to take hold. It was Fei Fei's mother. Her face was weary with pain.

"M-mom?" cried Fei Fei.

"Fei Fei," said her mother.

The diamond lights shifted and created a new image. Fei Fei at a younger age, grieving the loss of her mother. The girl knelt and hacked off her long hair with scissors while sobbing, wearing her loss for the world to see. *I am not whole. I am not the same as I was before.* The memory of losing her mother was too much for Fei Fei. She stumbled backward, crying out in pain before sinking to her knees. She curled into a ball.

Chang'e now found the strength to get up and move toward her. Her own concern for the young girl gave her strength. From the outside of the chamber, Fei Fei's friends tried to help her, to no avail. Gobi called to her, but she did not respond. Bungee tried to use her laser ears to break through the barrier. Chin ran into the barrier, crying Fei Fei's name. There was no use. They were all blocked out.

"I was afraid of this. She's stuck now," said Blue Lunette.

Chang'e and Fei Fei had changed positions. Chang'e was standing, and Fei Fei was the one curled up, unable to move. Chang'e nudged Fei Fei and saw her eyes open, filled with pain.

"You, what are you doing here? Wake up, you," said Chang'e sternly. "Why are you here? This is the Chamber of Exquisite Sadness. You don't belong here."

"But I do belong here," responded Fei Fei. Her voice was sad but certain.

"You can't stay here," said Chang'e. "You'll only end up lonely for all eternity, like me."

"But I am like you," said Fei Fei, still certain. She knew this with her whole being. Her father would marry Mrs. Zhong, and she would be alone.

"No, don't be like me," said Chang'e. She reached out and gently cupped Fei Fei's chin in her hand. "I won't let you stay here. You have to move on."

Fei Fei blinked, trying to understand. "How?" she asked. She wasn't asking how Chang'e was going to keep her from staying; she wanted to know how she was supposed to move on.

Chang'e took a deep breath. Sometimes where words alone might fail, music might succeed. She began to sing to Fei Fei, about the pain of loss but also letting love come through, to pursue a new life, if not the same life.

As Chang'e sang the song that she meant for

Fei Fei, the goddess realized that the same words applied to her. That even if she could not have the life she had before, she could have a life of love, more love than she imagined possible. Her eyes grew large and intent as she stared at the barrier before her.

If you can give love
You will find your family
Though it may not be
Like it was before
If you give love
You'll never lose love
It only grows—more and more

"Her spirit's always near," whispered Chang'e. "So trust that she will always be with you, and love someone new."

Now Fei Fei turned to look at the barrier, and saw Chin on the other side. She got up and began walking toward him, just as Chin began charging toward the wall, his face fierce with love. He let loose his battle cry one more time.

"No barriers!" he screamed. "I want my sister!"

In an instant, the barrier was shattered. Chin had passed through the wall and straight into Fei Fei's arms. The two embraced, clinging to each other. Love had let Chin through.

"Chin," said Fei Fei. "You saved me!" It was not clear who was more surprised by this—Fei Fei or Chin.

"Am I still a dingbat?" asked Chin, clearly hoping for an upgrade. He looked up into Fei Fei's eyes, seeking her approval.

Fei Fei thought a moment. "Yes," she said. "But you're *my* dingbat." The air was no longer so cold or unkind. Chin's hug warmed her. Life was beginning to flow back into her limbs, her heart, her brain. Suddenly, she could see opportunities and possibilities, not just loss and sadness.

Chin nodded, satisfied. "Can we go home now?" Running through barriers all the time was exhausting.

"Yeah," said Fei Fei. "Let's go home." But she had one more mission to take care of first. She turned to Chang'e.

"What about you?" she asked the goddess.

"I think it's too late for me," said Chang'e. "Houyi is not coming back." There was no temper in her voice, only sadness. Acceptance.

Fei Fei looked around the chamber and saw the Lunarians gathering around, trying to check on Chang'e. Chang'e might not have Houyi, but that did not mean she did not have love. Fei Fei returned her own message in song.

The gift is not the answer
And you are not alone
For love is all around you
A love you've always known
And though it hurts to miss him
His spirit's always near
The heart grows
And it knows

You can glow. . . .
You're wonderful

The song was part of another song, holding the wisdom that Gobi had shared with Fei Fei, and now she shared it with Chang'e. The goddess turned slowly to take in the scene, just outside the Chamber of Exquisite Sadness. Jade Rabbit. The Lunettes. The Lunarians. Even the palace guards. Gobi watched, unsure at first if he should approach the goddess. Then, throwing caution to the wind, he raced forward. Chang'e raised her eyebrows, not sure of what she was seeing after a thousand years.

"Gobi?"

Chang'e held her arms out to Gobi, but before Gobi could reach her, the rabbits, Blue Lunette, and all the Lunarians raced into her embrace, filling her arms in a tumble of arms, paws, scales, and crumbs. The emptiness she had been feeling could be filled if she was willing to let it happen. Gobi threw himself on Chang'e's feet; she reached down and hugged him, sending him into a happy glow. Gobi was home, back where he belonged.

The Chamber of Exquisite Sadness transformed into the Chamber of Exquisite Joy! Outside, in Lunaria, the lights popped back on, one by one, bringing light to all.

Chapter Twelve

"Fei Fei! Fei Fei! Fei Fei!" Her own name filled the air, rattling her ears. The happy crowd chanted Fei Fei's name as part of their celebration and then cheered as Chang'e emerged from the palace for the first time. The goddess looked genuinely happy, surrounded by Fei Fei and Chin, Gobi and the rabbits. The air filled with a symphony of rejoicing, laughter, and applause. A new era had begun in Lunaria. The goddess was ready to embrace and love her people with her whole heart; love was not meant for a precious few but for all who were present.

But then—it was time for goodbyes.

Gobi looked up at Fei Fei, his large eyes filling with tears. He was already trying to hang on to memories before she left, letting them rush out of his mouth. "Remember when we first met? Remember when you lassoed a frog with my tongue? Remember when we said goodbye?"

Fei Fei reached out and gently stroked her dear friend's face. "You mean, like right now?"

"Yes," said Gobi before bursting into tears. Fei Fei wrapped her arms around him, consoling him. This strange little creature had become a dear friend in a short time with his loyalty and patience. She promised to never forget him.

"Goodbye, Fei Fei," said Gobi as bravely as he could, once he had composed himself.

The rabbits were having a different kind of farewell. Jade Rabbit and Bungee huddled together, their ears flopping over one another. Fei Fei knelt down, and Bungee hopped over to her.

"Is this where you belong now?" Fei Fei asked tenderly. Bungee looked at Fei Fei, then Jade Rabbit, then back to Fei Fei. Fei Fei stroked the white rabbit's ears. Bungee licked her hand. They had been through so much together.

"I'll be okay," promised Fei Fei. "Go." She

watched Bungee race happily over to Jade Rabbit. "Goodbye, Bungee." Her eyes were misty. Jade Rabbit smooched Bungee on the cheek, and lasers shot out of her ears. That was enough to lift Fei Fei's spirits. She laughed, happy for her rabbit and her own discovery of love.

"Thank you for bringing me the gift, Fei Fei," said Chang'e, overlooking the crowd. She handed something to Fei Fei. The photo. "I hope you get what you are wishing for," said Chang'e regally.

Fei Fei accepted the photo happily. But then . . . something didn't feel right.

"I wish it had given you everything you wanted," said Fei Fei sincerely, thinking of the amulet.

"It did," said Chang'e slowly. "The real gift was you." Fei Fei felt her heart warm.

Chang'e made an elegant wave, beckoning to the winged lions. The lions flew down to the palace and then crouched at her feet. They were going to take Fei Fei and Chin home. The lions picked them up by their paws, lifting them into the air.

Gobi waved frantically. "Bye, Fei Fei! Besties forever! Forever! Chick-a chick-a forever! Forever!"

With one elegant leap, the lions began their flight.

The lunar landscape passed under them. They flew over Lunaria Lake, full of moon frogs. Croak waved to the frogs below. The moon grew smaller. Then, more deeply into space. A silvery, winged object flew by. A satellite.

Earth appeared in the distance. The twin lions moved to protect Fei Fei and Chin from the heat generated from reentering the atmosphere. Fei Fei took out the photo—the one of Chang'e that she had worked so hard to obtain. The photo caught fire, and Fei Fei slowly let it go, watching the flaming particles disappear into the stars. She felt peaceful. She didn't need the photo. She was going to be okay.

If anyone in the town had been awake at the moment that Fei Fei and Chin returned, they would have thought they saw a flaming meteor streak over the village, an orange blaze against the night sky. And if they had stayed awake a little longer, they would have seen a girl with choppy hair carrying a sleeping boy on her back, the very picture of a devoted older sister.

Fei Fei carried Chin over the bridge, stopping to pet one of the stone lions on the nose. A light glowed from the house, revealing a figure sitting on the dock. Baba was waiting for her. He had been waiting for her all along.

Even though clocks and calendars measure time at the same steady beat, the heart measures time differently. So much has happened in a year, from one Moon Festival to another—how could it only be a year? How could so much change fit into twelve months?

A puppy, for one thing. The tawny pup tumbled through the kitchen, amid family members getting ready for another celebration. "Outta the way, Space Dog!" chirped Fei Fei. She led him to his bed in the corner, and he chomped on the pillow.

The photos on the mantel showed even more

changes. A wedding photo of Baba and Mrs. Zhong. And Chin, with his ever-present Ping-Pong paddle. This time, though, he had a third-place prize, not fourth! And there was a photo of Fei Fei, her mother, and Baba because love does not forget. Love remembers and expands. Space is limitless, and so is love.

Some things stay the same. Grandpa stood in the middle of the kitchen, expounding once again on the merits of the hairy crab. "Eating hairy crabs has been called a life-changing experience!" he announced to anyone who would listen.

Fei Fei joined Mrs. Zhong in the kitchen, making mooncakes. "Zhong Ayi," she said, now calling her stepmother by the more familiar title of auntie, rather than Mrs. Zhong. "Can I try one of yours?"

"Oh! Well, of course!" Zhong Ayi made room for Fei Fei, and the two stood shoulder to shoulder, spreading flour on the wooden cutting board. The light caught Zhong Ayi's necklace and glittered; she was wearing her amulet.

"You know," said Zhong Ayi. "The Moon Festival is my favorite night of the year. My nai nai always told me the circle of the mooncake is the symbol of a family coming together." Fei Fei watched the woman knead her own ball of pastry, her hands moving in a way that was both familiar and new. This was their new tradition, together, connecting past, present, and future.

When it was time for dinner, Baba and Zhong Ayi patted the seat between them.

"Fei Fei, sit here," said Baba.

"Come sit by us," said Zhong Ayi.

But before Fei Fei could sit down, Croak leaped into the chair.

"Chin . . . ," called Fei Fei warningly.

Zhong Ayi was less patient. "Chin! Get that frog off the chair!" Chin poked his head out from under the table.

"Sorry!" Chin grabbed Croak, and Fei Fei sat down. Her grandparents, aunties, and uncle also joined them at the table.

Grandma looked out toward the night sky. It was a cloudy night. "It's the Moon Festival and no moon!" she said, disappointed.

"Chang'e must be so sad, hidden behind those clouds," said Auntie Mei, getting a soft look on her face. "Dreaming of her one true love."

"Oh, come on!" said Auntie Ling. "Don't start that again!"

"Start what?" asked Auntie Mei. "It's romantic!"

Fei Fei looked around the table, at her family, seeing both how normal and special it all was. *Pass me the crabs! More rice!* The gentle bickering and teasing, the same stories being passed around. Chin building a tower of dumplings. And yet, it was all special because they were together. Grandpa spun the lazy Susan, trying to get to his precious crabs and missing. Fei Fei caught the spinning tray and gently turned the crabs back to her grandfather.

The clouds eventually parted, letting the moon appear. The moon was in the sky and in the water.

Fei Fei took in the quiet moment by herself at the canal; then Baba joined her on the dock.

"Looks like the moon has decided to come out for us after all," he said. "What do you think Jade Rabbit's making tonight?"

Fei Fei leaned into her father. "Moooon mush."

"Moooon mush," repeated Baba. Then they both laughed, Fei Fei's laugh turning into a snort.

"You laugh just like your mama," said Baba. Fei Fei's heart fluttered at hearing him say "Mama." It had been a long time since Baba had said her name out loud.

"I know," said Fei Fei. She closed her eyes and remembered her mother's laugh, and the memory filled her heart.

"Should we head back?" asked Baba.

"I'll be right there," said Fei Fei. She looked up at the moon, letting the night be magical and quiet. The moon was huge and full. She took off her scarf, the one with Chang'e on it, and held it out so she could see it better. The light from the moon illuminated the details on the scarf—Chang'e gesturing in her elegant robes and Jade Rabbit working among swirling clouds.

A whoosh passed behind her. The flapping of wings. It was a giant crane, elegant and white. It glided onto a post at the end of the dock and then turned to look at Fei Fei. Fei Fei sat up, startled by the bird. The crane looked directly at her with kind eyes and then cocked its head, like a greeting.

As Fei Fei retied the scarf around her neck, the crane took off, its wide wings spreading over the water. The rush of its wings was so strong it ruffled her hair. Fei Fei laughed softly to herself, wondering if anyone would believe what just had happened.

Then—a Ping-Pong ball bounced off her head.

"Urgh!" grunted Fei Fei. The magical moment was broken, by the world's most annoying—and wonderful—little brother.

"Hahaha!" cried Chin, running away as fast as his short legs would allow.

Fei Fei chased after him. "All right, you ding-bat!" shouted Fei Fei.

"Mo-om! Fei Fei's chasing me!" tattled Chin as he darted back toward the house.

"No I'm not!" said Fei Fei. But she laughed so her parents would know she was joking.

"Chin! Stop chasing your sister," scolded Zhong Ayi, who had a better idea of the truth.

"Fei Fei!" called Baba.

The sounds of their happy voices crisscrossed and carried through the night, up into the air . . . and maybe all the way to the moon?